Arthur H. Winnington Ingram

The Brides of Dinan

A Tale of the Barons' War, in Six Cantos

Arthur H. Winnington Ingram

The Brides of Dinan
A Tale of the Barons' War, in Six Cantos

ISBN/EAN: 9783337080327

Printed in Europe, USA, Canada, Australia, Japan

Cover: Foto ©Andreas Hilbeck / pixelio.de

More available books at **www.hansebooks.com**

THE BRIDES OF DINAN.

THE BRIDES OF DINAN.

A TALE OF THE BARONS' WAR.

In Six Cantos.

BY

ARTHUR H. WINNINGTON INGRAM,

HONORARY CANON OF WORCESTER CATHEDRAL,
RECTOR OF HARVINGTON, ETC., ETC.

LONDON:

GEORGE BELL AND SONS, YORK STREET,

COVENT GARDEN.

1888.

CHISWICK PRESS :—C. WHITTINGHAM AND CO., TOOKS COURT,
CHANCERY LANE.

TO HIS WIFE

THIS POEM IS DEDICATED

BY

THE AUTHOR.

NOTICE TO THE PUBLIC.

THE gifted and learned author of this poem was suddenly called away before his work (the delight of his leisure hours for some years) was prepared for the press.

He left several copies of it, written out at different times, each varying from the others frequently in detail, all entirely unpunctuated, and with innumerable pencil corrections, many of which have been very difficult, and some of them impossible, to decipher.

The editor therefore fears she may not in numerous instances have done justice to, nor given accurately, her husband's poetical ideas; but, having performed her labour of love in the best way she could, she must leave it to the kindness of the reader to excuse all defects on her part.

S. M. W. I.

Long Hyde, Littleton, Evesham.
September, 1888.

AUTHOR'S PREFACE.

THE action of the poem, which the Author believes to be a correct exponent of the manners and feelings of the age in which its scene is laid, commences on May 28th, 1265, with a wolf-hunt in the neighbourhood of Ludlow, formerly called Dinan, a name corrupted from Dinham, or Dena ham, the residence of the Danes. Readers may perhaps be surprised at such a chase being introduced into the story, but indisputable records inform us that England was about that period so much infested with wolves, that in the next reign, that of Edward I., a royal mandate was issued to Peter Corbett, that in all forests, parks, and other places in the counties of Worcester, Gloucester, Hereford, Salop, and Stafford, in which he might find wolves, he was to hunt the same with men, dogs, and engines, to destroy them.

After a description of the events connected with the escape of Prince Edward from Hereford, the narrative is suspended for about two months, and then continued on August 2nd, 1265, concluding with the occurences of August 6th in the same year. The Author is anxious that his historical romance should not lead to a confusion of authentic facts with poetical fictions, and so advertises his readers, that while in delineating the characters of Henry III., Prince Edward, Simon de Montfort, and other principal persons, and giving an account of the battle of Evesham, and the events immediately preceding that momentous struggle, he has conscientiously endeavoured to reconcile the conflicting statements of the contemporary monastic chroniclers, and keep to historical truth. The visit of the Earl of Leicester to Wigmore Castle on the day when his nephew Prince Edward arrived there from Hereford is hypothetical, and the courtship of Isabel by Henry Montfort (called by the monk of Lanercost " Impubes miles et virgo innocens "), the bethrothal of Sir Walter Croft (styled in the Monasticon the Lord of Croft) to Margaret, the devotion of Llewellyn to the same, and the development of these romantic attachments, are creations of the Author's imagination. The ballad sung by Isabel is a free poetical version of a prose story in the Anglo-Norman romance of the Fitz-Warines, relating to the adventures of Fulk Fitz-Warine in the previous reign of King John. The scene of the poem is laid at Ludlow and Wigmore Castles, the Cistercian convent of Lymbroke, and the battle-field of Evesham.

CONTENTS.

PAGE

CANTO I.
The Wolf-Hunt 1

CANTO II.
Wigmore Castle 37

CANTO III.
The Abbey of Lymbroke 58

CANTO IV.
The March 86

CANTO V.
The Battle of Evesham 100

CANTO VI.
The Marriage 152

THE BRIDES OF DINAN.

CANTO I.

THE WOLF-HUNT.

LORD Genville heard the hunter's call
   Resound before his castle gate,
And to the court paced from the hall,
With followers in feudal state;
The Baron's daughter, at the blast,
After her sire, with light step pass'd,
And near her fretful palfrey stay'd,
That guidance of a groom obey'd,
And the glad concourse she survey'd.
Varlets, who track the game to lairs,
Are in the yard, and foresters
Keep the strong wiry hounds in check,
Straining against the leash, the neck;
And grooms hold steeds that stamp and snort,
Impatient for the sylvan sport.

But she herself in bloom of days
And loveliness allured the gaze
Of one, who 'mid the huntsmen stood;
His hand held spear of tough ash-wood,

B

And at his side hung silver horn.
Tall as a fir-tree tower'd his height,
His eye with youthful fire shone bright,—
He was Earl Leicester's eldest born.
His handsome countenance might move
The coldest damsel's soul to love;
And as he look'd upon the maid,
In huntress' light costume array'd,
In tunic white, and mantle blue,
And mark'd her locks of glossy hue,
The colour of the raven's pinion,
Shadow her soft and beauteous cheek,
His heart that lov'd her, grew more meek,
And own'd her beauty's strong dominion.

De Genville, of his spouse bereft,
Had been with this one daughter left,
Heiress of all his land;
Rich meadows by the side of Teme,
And Corve, and Onny's sounding stream,
Would dower the maiden's hand;
And many a wooer sought in vain
Her beauty and her wealth to gain;
But she knew love alone by name,
Nor felt as yet the wasting flame;
And joy'd, thro' woods, to urge the chase
Of deer, or wolf, at rapid pace;
Setting slight store by her fair face;
And all unoccupied, and lone,
Remain'd her bosom's envied throne.

But ah ! she is of age when soon
Her heart may beat to love's sweet tune ;
So Henry Montfort her address'd :
" Good morrow, lady, all is fair
For the wild sport we come to share ; "
And love was in his tone express'd.
" But where is now thy sire, our guest ? "
She ask'd him with a careless air.
" His knees yon chapel-pavement press ;
Prayer makes, he says, the day no longer,
But for its work the spirit stronger ;
We feel our labour less."

When Henry answer'd, mass was o'er,
And Leicester, through an open door,
(Conducting from the inner close,
Where chapel round and solid rose,)
In hunting garb appear'd.
The company their brows made bare,
He rais'd the cap from his white hair ;
And loud, the vassals cheer'd ;
For all maintain'd a firm belief,
In the great merit of their chief ;
Strong built, and of gigantic mould,
His frame well match'd his spirit bold.
In tunic green the Earl was clad,
And in his hand a lance he had ;
A worn look show'd upon his face,
Of midnight meditation, trace ;
And, on his forehead's broad expanse,

All could perceive a forge of thought,
Where many a sage design was wrought
In England and in France ;
And had been plann'd full many a chart
Of battle, with consummate art,
To check his foes' advance.

Came with the Earl, Lord Cantelupe,
Of stately form, and noble face,
Accoutred also for the chase,
And join'd the social troop ;
No prelate more revered than he,
Wise ruler of fair Worcester's see ;
Him, priestly crew in honour bore,
His counsel too was sought in war,
He studied much the ancient lore ;
But held not woodland sport in scorn,
And lov'd to follow hound and horn.

As Leicester paced the court along
Toward his coal-black courser strong,
The lord of Dinan coldly gave
A greeting to the leader brave,
Who check'd his march, and made reply,—
" Deem it not lack of courtesy
That I thy sport delay'd ;
For oh ! how could I bear the weight
Of all the grave affairs of state,
By which the soul is oft dismay'd,—
Guidance of men, in arms array'd,

And managing of many things
That fall to counsellors of kings,—
Unless to God I pray'd.
I love to hear the humble friars,
Chant praises in their holy choirs,
It soothes my weary careworn heart,
And strengthens me to bear the part
That my high place requires."

" I am besieg'd by rebel aims,
And treachery my caution claims ;
But, by the arm of holy James,
Since it is now King Henry's will
That I the post of ruler fill,
I may not slacken in my hand
The reins he gave me of command."
And then he cast a look upon
The Earl of Hereford's brave son :—
" Bohun, thou shalt this day be spared
From our attendance, to be guard
Of good King Henry; he loves well
The lively chase o'er moor and fell ;
But in this week of Pentecost,
Would not, from Church, an hour were lost.
I left him in the Chapel there,
Still kneeling on the stone in prayer ;
His piety I reverence ;—
So, while to slay the beast we toil,
That snatches from the sheep-fold, spoil,
Remain for his defence."

Bohun his head in answer bow'd,
And, mourning loss of forest sport,
Departed from the cheerful crowd
To chapel of the fort.

Lord Genville bit his lip, and hate
Did on his forehead lower ;
But he submitted to the fate
That gave De Montfort power ;
And said, "Come, let us now forget
The cares whereby we are beset,
In sport, this morning hour.
The monks of Bromfield oft complain,
A skulking wolf their lambs hath ta'en,
And we from coursing him refrain ;
And what of lord and knight the use
If they the war or chase refuse ?"
" It is not well we longer stay,"
Lord Bishop Cantelupe did say ;
" While with your brethren ye have feud,
The wolves increase in multitude ;
Such should by you be slain,
Else refuges must soon be made,
Where travellers through the forest-shade
May in the night remain.
To chase these plagues is better far
Than breaking heads and helms in war ;
Huntsmen have little time for sin,
When once the hounds the cry begin."

Lord Genville's bugle call'd to horse,
To mount, and the fierce wolf to course;
Toward his steed his steps he bends,
And Leicester to his charger wends.
He stroked his dark and glossy hide,
And mounted him, whose nostrils wide
Snorted and breath'd forth clouds of steam,
White glimmering in the morning beam.
And Worcester's lordly prelate too
Bestrode his courser, that well knew
The hand above his waving mane,
Checking his fire with broider'd rein ;
And 'neath his honour'd burden proud,
Filled all the court with neighing loud.

When Isabel approach'd her steed,
Young Montfort did her purpose heed,
And swiftly ran the rein to hold,
That she to mount might be more bold ;
And, witch'd by her dark beaming eyes,
Address'd her thus, in gentle guise :
" I hope my sire here long may stay
That we, together, oft may stray,
And so make short a summer day ; "
She, with a word, replied ;
Then turning, did her glances bend
Upon a modest gentle friend,
Standing her steed beside.

She wore a tunic of the hue
We in the sky unclouded view ;

Tender and graceful was her form ;
Her steps, as light as rose-leaves' fall,
Scarce seem'd to press the turf at all ;
Her heart with sympathy was warm,
And so the maiden came to say,
She wish'd her friend a happy day.
Pure thoughts did in her bosom dwell,
As nun's, within a cloister'd cell.
Her auburn hair and clear blue eye
Bespoke a Saxon ancestry ;
Of them who dwelt about the place,
Not one her parentage could trace ;
Her years of girlhood had been pass'd
Where Idris rears his masses vast,
In a strong castle, near the fountain
Of Arthog's stream, beneath the mountain.
Llys Bradwen's lord, two years ago,
One eve to Dinan's Castle brought her,
And pray'd Lord Genville to bestow
On his adopted daughter
An education fair and meet,
To make her life and converse sweet ;
So, nurtured with his Isabel,
She did in Dinan's fortress dwell.
The maidens were call'd "Morn" and "Night,"
For one had dark hair, one had light.
The beauty of the morn,
Jewell'd with dew in early spring,
When all the birds begin to sing,
Did Margaret adorn ;

And summer night's soft loveliness
Might well her friend's sweet charms express.

If Isabel knew naught of love,
That passion did her friend's heart move.
The son of Bradwen's Chief had tried,
In vain, to win her as his bride;
But on all blandishments she frown'd;
Yet lately, in lone Whitcliffe wood,
While sauntering in a careless mood,
A heart to beat with hers had found.
She lov'd the stripling at first view;
Something mysterious seem'd to draw
The two together, more and more,
And every day they fonder grew.
When came the tranquil evening hour,
And the soft pearls fell on the flower,
Hand link'd in hand, they oft were seen,
By the light fairies on the green;
And, when the stars, like God's own eyes,
Look'd on them from the darken'd skies,
They pass'd some stainless hours of love,
Straying together through the grove;
But no one in the Castle knew
They held such loving interview.

"So thou wilt in the fort remain,
And join not the glad hunting train,"
Said Isabel unto the maid,
Who still beside her palfrey stay'd;

But answer'd her, the damsel good,
"To drive the wolf through brake and wood
Is not according to my mood ;
If in the chase my steed I strain,
I think of the poor quarry's pain ;
He dreads to hear the sound of horn
Behind him on the breezes borne ;
And all my wishes are that he
May of his barking foes be free :
Or when a heron, pierced by beak
Of falcon, hurtles from the sky,—
(It may appear to thee but weak,—)
A tear starts in my eye.
I now unto the pleasance go,
Some flower-seeds in the soil to sow,
And sweet-pea round our arbour train,
And tulips tall with rods sustain,
Lest they be beaten down by rain ;
And then, perhaps, my glance may stray
O'er Merlin and King Arthur's lay."

"Thou alway wilt thy time employ
In tasks that yield a gentle joy ;
I think, ere many months have run,
Thou wilt profess thyself a nun :
Farewell sweetheart, we meet at eve."
So Isabel of her took leave :
Then grasping firm the glossy mane,
She did her palfrey's saddle gain.
A wolf-hound, full of joy and love,

Longing to be by her caress'd,
Leap'd up, and lick'd her jewell'd glove,
Her hand his forehead press'd.

Young Henry, envious of the hound
That had such gracious favour found,
Brisk vaulted to his courser's selle,
And in the sight of Isabel,
Spurr'd his steed's flank, and waved his whip,
And show'd his skilful horsemanship.
A cup of red wine from the South
Pass'd quickly round from mouth to mouth ;
The horn again, pluck'd from his belt,
The lip of Dinan's Baron felt,
And sent forth note of cheerful force,
Welcome to man, and hound, and horse ;
And all the jovial cavalcade
Rode forth for sport in sylvan glade.
They pass'd the moat by wooden bridge,
And hasten'd on, to Whitcliffe ridge.
The fields were full of joy that morn,
New life in everything was born ;
The cuckoo flew from bower to bower,
(A wandering and embodied song,)
Bloom'd on the meads the cowslip flower,
And celandine, the stream along.

On Bringewood Hill the uncoupled hounds
Dart off with eager, joyous bounds,
Through golden gorses of the fell

To lovely Downton's yew-clad dell.
The mountain sinks so steep and sheer
To Teme's swift silvery ripple clear,
That, as believ'd by simple swain,
The gorge through which the waters flow
Was cloven by the mighty blow
Of sword of giant Dane.
The pack ran through the dismal glen,
Meet spot for wild beasts' bone-strewn den ;
There, in a cave 'mid crags and stubs,
A huge grey wolf had hid his cubs,
And soon a lym-dog's voice reveal'd
Where the fierce miscreant was conceal'd ;
He cast one look toward his lair,
The dam and tawny young ones there,
And started on the fearful race,
His life depending on the chase.

Hark ! to the wolf-hounds' joyful cries,
Hark ! how the crags with ivy hung
Echo the pack with softer tongue,
And give back faint replies.
At first the chase broke slowly through
The thicket, and the hill-side copse,
And where they brush'd the bough, the dew
Fell down in silvery drops ;
From the dark covert fled the deer,
And scour'd the hill in frantic fear,
And through the wood ran to and fro,
Shrinking from bay of hound, the doe.

But the staunch pack pursued the beast
That made upon the lambs his feast;
The huntsmen had no time to view
The hyacinths' rich carpet blue;
Or wild and white anemones
Mantle the root of hoary trees;
Or ferns, their brittle feathery scroll,
In the May morning bright unroll;
Or primroses, with pale gold dress
Robe mossy bank; but on they press.

Clear of the wood, o'er grassy plain
They gallop'd swift with loosen'd rein,
And saw the Teme's pure waters twine
In many a maze from Leintwardine.
Resounded soon their horses' tramp,
Where, gathering once at trumpet-call,
Rome's legions mann'd the turfy wall
Of Brandon's deep-trench'd camp.
And then, the guard on Brampton tower
Beheld them crush the cowslip flower,
On mead, his rampart near;
And Stanage!—thy birch-waving hill,
Whose charms work in my memory still,—
Echoed the bugle blowing shrill,
That urged their swift career.

The quarry thought the Teme to swim,
So hot the hunter's pressed on him,
And find in fissure deep, a port,

Where lofty crags of Holloway
Uprear'd their ivied masses grey,
Of old his loved resort ;
But close upon his track, a hound,
With muzzle lifted from the ground,
Keeping the prey in sight,
Turn'd the fierce prowler, that he slunk
By dingle on the hillside sunk,
To Reeve's bleak airy height.
The huntsman scaled the deep ravine,
Where oaks were budding into green,
And saw the roamer quite at fault,
Sniffing about the fern, and bent
To find again the failing scent,
And on the summit halt.

As there they stay'd their coursers fleet,
What prospects fair their glances greet !
Below, embower'd in birchen-copse,
And sentinell'd by mountain tops,
(Rich yellow gorses crowning them,
Like kings, with golden diadem,)
Reclines the town of Tref-y-clawdd ;[1]
And, as bright links of silver, gleam
The windings of the pebbly Teme ;
A lovely scene they all allow'd ;
And Henry said, " The hills and vales
Upon the border land of Wales,
If woke the voice of minstrelsy

[1] Knighton.

To sing their legendary tales,
Might well with Scotland's marches vie."

Quoth Genville, " Still are unforgot
The deeds done here : observe yon spot,
That wall of ivy-mantled rock,
From whence the weary wolf we turn'd ;
There, British valour fiercely burn'd,
When the strong Roman legions' shock
Compell'd to flight bold Caradoc;
And Celtic lance met Latin pile,
And all these hills that stand about
Resounded with the battle shout
Of the last champions of our Isle."
" O yes ! the scene may well excite
The valour of a chivalrous knight
To win his lady's smile,"
Said Henry, casting fervent look
On Isabel's sweet countenance ;
But her cold bosom could not brook
His earnest, searching glance.
" Look now at Hereford's fair shire,"
Said she, to turn his gaze away ;
" That verdant track I more admire
From Shobdon hill to heathery Hay ;
In valley green and wooded knoll
Like emerald waves it seems to roll
Of some bright ocean bay."
But Leicester's noble Earl replied,
" Yon shire yields pasturage to keep

Large flocks of those soft fleecèd sheep,
Brought from Morena's thorny steep
By Edward's Spanish bride."

But hark ! beside that grassy mound
Which Offa's kingdom once did bound,
A staunch and busy dog of chase
Hath sniff'd the weary victim's trace,
And soon the bugle's cheerful strain
Announced the scent was found again.
The thong then smites the courser's flank,
And huntsmen now descend the bank,
And, hurrying with the cry, post on
By fort-crown'd hill of Stapleton ;
Their course lay through a valley spread
With forest, where the wild roe bred,
And from the oak-trees' airy height
Clapp'd the blue cushat's wing in flight.
With merry noise they briskly drove
The plunderer from grove to grove ;
And oft he led the hound and horn
From out the covert's shady place
To where from wood was clear'd a space,
And clad with springing corn.
But thinking of his hungry brood,
In cavern foul, with bones and blood,
The wily brute desired to wind,
'Twixt wooded hills that closely hug
The crystal waters of the Lug,
To Downton, and his old haunt find.

But headed by a chance-met swain,
He turn'd upon his path again;
And all the baffled chasers took
Toward the thorns of Boultibrook;
There, hoping to destroy the scent
That from his reeking hide did steam,
He paddled up a stony stream,
But foil'd was his intent.

The victors, 'neath a beetling rock,
Bayed at the waster of the flock,
And close environ'd him about,
And volley'd their fierce anger out,
To make the monster fear;
The glen was horrible with sound
Of snarl of wolf, and yell of hound,
That came his tusk too near;
And, as to tear the throat he sprang,
Felt in his hide the pointed fang,
And paid for rashness dear.
Already had the sharp teeth stream'd
With blood, from three staunch hounds unseam'd,
When Henry reach'd the ground,
And saw deep tusk, and fiery eyes,
Defy the yelling enemies;
And sought the wretch to wound.

He, from his steed, lanced at the neck,
And made the purple blood to spurt;
But dreading lest some hound be hurt,

The spear awhile did check ;
And making aim more sure, sent point
Deeply into the shoulder joint.
The tortured savage tore the wood
With angry tusks, and then the blood
Far up the spear-shaft gleam'd.
The hunter drew the lance away,
And smote once more the monster grey,
Again the red blood stream'd ;
He snapp'd his jaws, and tried to tear
Forth from the crimson wound, the spear,
And on the mosses sank.
The youth awaited till had ceas'd
The writhing of the wounded beast,
Whose blood the green earth drank ;
And when he lay bereft of life,
Drove the tormentors from the dead,
And, quick dismounting, with a knife
Hew'd off the grisly head,
And wav'd it, while with boisterous noise
The leaping wolf-hounds bark'd their joys.

O'er the dumb prey was blown the pryse,
When, heated with her exercise,
Came Isabel alone ;
Alone, the foremost of the chase,
She sat her jaded steed with grace,
And ne'er more lovely seem'd her face,
The dark locks round it blown.
" Thou should'st have check'd thy woodland craft,

Nor dyed with blood the lance's haft,
Till I arriv'd to mark the death
Of game that tax'd our coursers' breath."
Thus spoke she, measuring with her eyes
The sprawling monster's wondrous size.
But Henry said, "The angry brute
Might have sprung up and maim'd thy foot ;
It is not meet for lady fair
To face a hunted wolf's despair ;
Thou art with other triumphs crown'd,
And with thy glance can young hearts wound."
Then, at these words, a look of scorn
Her lovely visage did adorn.

Sad thoughts young Montfort's soul convulse,
At repetition of repulse.
"In vain I try to win her love ;
Cold as the goddess of the chase
Was fabled by the Grecian race,
She meets me with relentless face,
No words her heart can move ;
I shall obtain her love as soon
As child who wimpers for the moon
May win that high and golden boon."
Now Leicester on his tall dark steed
Approaching, lauded Henry's deed ;
But to himself the young knight says,
"Oh! much I should prefer *her* praise,
Whose cheek the wanton wind caresses,

Playing among her glossy tresses;
But me, with not one smile she blesses."

After the Earl, Lord Cantelupe
Rode up, and others join'd the troop.
" Our horses' necks are white with foam,
Their flanks are plaster'd o'er with loam,
Of soil of many a different hue,
Which all day long we gallopp'd through.
The foot-sore hounds can hardly creep,
With drooping tail the heath they sweep;
Some shake the tatter'd ear for pain,
Some lick from wounded part, the stain.
See, how they loll the scarlet tongue,
To give relief to panting lung.
The sun doth in the heaven descend,
The shadows of the trees extend;
The strongest huntsman needs repast
After the long day's chase and fast;
Say, is there not some castle near,
Or abbey, where we may find cheer?"
To Dinan's lord, so Leicester spoke,
Curbing his steed beneath an oak.

But Genville answer'd, " Fair Presteign,
Not far beyond that meadow green,
Sends up its evening cloud of smoke;
And Stapleton's strong fort of war
Will not against us close the door;
And towers of Lingen, too, are nigh;

And south of them, in Lymbroke's dell,
There is of nuns a little cell,
But they to help us will be shy.
In Wigmore's hall is store of food ;"
Then, thrusting forth a hunting spear
Towards some knolls, thick set with wood,
" Behind yon haunts of wild red deer,"
He said, " the castle stood."
" Thither," quoth Montfort, " be our guide
Through mazes of the forest wide,
For though his dame at us may scold
Sir Roger will not help withhold."

Upon Croft Ambrey's deep-trench'd height
Linger'd the farewell evening light,
And tinged the copse upon the wold
With glorious breadth of shadowy gold,
When Montfort drew his courser's rein
An arrow's flight from Wigmore's moat,
Announcing by a bugle note
The presence of his train.
The bridge hung poised, the gate was barr'd,
And with a spiked portcullis sparr'd ;
But on the height of barbican
A solitary guard did scan
The troop outside that stay'd ;
His gaze inquir'd if they were those
Whom he awaited, or were foes,
And strictly them survey'd.
An angry look De Montfort sent,

And blew a loud and startling tone,
Which brought between each battlement
An aged man with cross-bow bent,—
For age was there alone ;
Manhood and youth, with Wigmore's lord,
At dawn of day had march'd abroad,
On quest to them unknown.

Earl Leicester saw the bowmen stoop,
And bend their yews in embrazure,
That they might take and aim more sure
At him, and his small troop ;
And, in return for hostile act,
Desired, by threatening note of horn,
The chain of drawbridge to be slack'd,
And the portcullis' spike updrawn,
Or they would rouse his scorn.
But when the guard, who still did peer,
The Earl's demands declined to hear,
He spurr'd his weary steed more near ;
And spake, while frowns his forehead cloud :
" Let not the King's vicegerent wait ;
Lower the bridge, fling wide the gate,
Or else look for a rebel's fate,
Hung from yon turret proud."
A clank upon the watch-tower stairs
Compliance with his hest declares ;
The bridge fell thund'ring o'er the trench,
And heav'd by trusty warders' wrench,
The spiked portcullis rose.

And weary hound, and hunters' rank,
Moved slowly o'er the rumbling plank,
Thro' arch, whose gates unclose.
They enter'd, and faced in the court
The haughty mistress of the fort.
She wore a tunic, purple dyed,
And saffron mantle, flowing wide,
That 'neath the neck with link was tied
Of brooch and golden band ;
Her features hard betray'd a heart
Where cruelty and lust had part,
With love of high command.
On them, who, by her vassals caught,
Were to her dismal dungeon brought,
Inhuman vengeance oft she wrought.
But with the magic of her smile,
Could hearts of innocence beguile—
Had mov'd Prince Edward's heart erewhile ;
And since he had been captive made,
She took the royal stripling's part,
And sought by many a wily art
His wish'd escape to aid.

" Pardon, high dame, if we intrude,
We crave this evening rest and food,"
Said Leicester, who his wrath subdued.
"Altho' now absent is my lord,
There's forage for your steeds in stall,
And venison for your feast in hall,
And wine in cellar stor'd."

Dissembling thus to him her hate,
She led her guests to hall, where late
Hung deadly weapons meet for war ;
But gone were battleaxe and blade,
And armour that brave knights array'd ;
Yet on the walls were still display'd
Of tokens of the chase, a store ;—
Cross-bow, and spear, that wolf defied,
Whose grim grey head the stone-walls bore,
And skull of deer with antlers wide,
And white-tusk'd jowl of boar.

A goodly feast she had prepared,
Her husband's glad return to greet ;
No cost nor trouble had been spar'd
To load the board with meat ;
And, since to stay the Earl she sought,
She bade the banquet to be brought,
And in her heart indulg'd the thought
That when her lord return'd,
The haughty ruler would be taught
And given the meed he earn'd.
The feast was on the table laid,
And round it were the guests array'd.
From Wigmore's lake, broad carp and bream,
And speckl'd trout from silvery Teme,
Haunches of red deer, kill'd with bolt,
And hams of wild swine, spear'd in holt,
Sent up from trenchers savoury steam.

Fair Isabel sate at the daïs,
And with a beamsome smiling face
Talk'd with dame Maud about the chase,
But of Sir Henry took no heed,
Although his gaze for love did plead.
When Bordeaux wine and gen'rous food
The hunters' hunger had subdued,
Lord Genville thus the Earl address'd :
" Shall we our hostess now request
To let us here till morning rest ? "
De Montfort answer'd, " Noble knight,
This evening by the young moon's light
I to thy fortress will return ;
And mean to-morrow morn to bring
To Hereford again, the King ;
And, with my own keen eye, discern
If good De Ros take proper care
Of the bold Prince, my captive there.
I to my nephew have been kind,
And his request have not denied
A race with his young guards to ride,—
But flight may be design'd ;
He may this privilege abuse,
And, for escape, the occasion choose :
The Psalmist bids us to accord
No faith in any prince's word."

Without the gate a horn was wound ;
The dogs that weary limbs had laid
On rush-strewn floor, woke up and bay'd ;

The sparkling cup ceas'd circling round ;
The guest who held the cup to mouth
Withdrew it, ere he quench'd his drouth.
The strangers seated in the hall
Wonder'd who did the warder call,
But 'twas well known to Lady Maud,
Whose breath the curling horn did fill,
That sounded at the gateway shrill ;—
She knew it was her lord,
And was most eager, too, to learn
How sped his secret enterprise,
And to the door she turn'd her eyes,
His entrance to discern.

The mystery was quickly solv'd,
For on the hinge the door revolv'd,
And, marshall'd by a seneschal,
The Castle's lord—Sir Mortimer—
In armour soil'd from helm to spur,
With cheerful look, paced up the hall.
But, oh ! the gladdest sight of all,
She saw, close at her husband's side,
A youthful knight, both straight and tall,
Approach with haughty stride ;
Whose tresses long of auburn hair
Hung down beside his visage fair ;
His mantle blue, befoul'd with mud,
Shows he his courser's speed had strain'd,
And with fresh crimson spots of blood
His habergeon is stain'd.

And in the glare of torches' flame
Behind him band of soldiers came.
With eye as piercing as a hawk's,
Gazing around, he onward stalks ;
But when on Montfort fell his glance,
Gather'd upon his brow a gloom,
Yet forward still his steps advance,
To place of honour in the room.
Whispers went round, " It is the Prince ;"
Some fear, some reverence evince ;
The hunters at each other stared,
Surprise was in their look declared,

Earl Simon felt his falchion's hilt,
And cried, " Hast thou to former guilt
To add another trespass dared,
And hither come, without thy guard ? "
In Edward's face the red wrath burn'd,
And he De Montfort's taunt return'd :
"Thanks to King Edward, my good Saint,
And to my trusty lance and sword,
And help of yon kind lady's lord,
I'm free from thy restraint.
Yes, to thy face, I say I'm free,
And will maintain my liberty ;
And since I am once more at large,
I, of this fort, assume the charge."
Then to Sir Roger turn'd a look,
And said, " I bid thee to arrest
Here in thy hall thy rebel guest ;

I wonder how thy spouse could brook
To let him in her castle rest.
Proud uncle! now the time is come
When thou must yield the masterdom."
When such intent his words disclose,
Montfort and all the hunters rose.
"And this means war," Earl Leicester cried,
And pluck'd the falchion from his side;
The others mutter'd threatening words,
And from the scabbard drew their swords.

This rous'd of Wigmore's men the blood,
To see their Prince's hest withstood;
And, waiting not their lord's commands,
They fiercely rush'd with rapid pace
Toward the Baron at the daïs,
To seize and put him into bands.
But Henry Montfort forward stepp'd,
And from the sheath his falchion drew;
It round in fearful circles swept,
And from his sire the weapons kept,
Of all the hostile crew.
But then the voice of Maud arose,
And fann'd the wrath of Leicester's foes:
"Strike, seize the traitor on the spot,
Cast him into our keep to rot,
Or lead him to our watch-tower's height,
And give his giant body flight,
That it may dash upon the stones,
And our fierce wolf-hounds gnaw his bones."

The shrill tone of her voice agreed
With passions that for vengeance plead,—
It echoed through the hall;
The fluttering hawks on perches scream'd,
The soldiers' weapons whirl'd, and gleam'd
In torch-light, and red blood had stream'd
In fierce and angry brawl,
If Mortimer had not in haste,
Betwixt his men and Leicester, placed
His form, like stedfast oak.
"O! hearken not unto my wife,
Who in my hall would fan the strife;
O my brave Prince! withdraw command
That I on Leicester lay my hand;
He will not yield without a stroke,
And I must not stain with his gore
My hospitable mansion's floor;
In open battle when we meet,
I will not from his sword retreat."

These words Prince Edward's wrath appease;
He now revoked command to seize
The haughty Earl; "Quite soon enough;
The time will come to try the stuff
Of our stout hearts in contest tough,
So banish hate awhile."
Said Mortimer, "Your hearts incline
To mirth, and sport, and purple wine,
And harpers singing songs divine,
That turn the frown to smile."

Earl Leicester, who not once had quail'd
When by the threatening steel assail'd,
Thus sternly answer'd Mortimer:
" Although thy words have striven to tame
The fury of thy cruel dame,
Thy shelter I no longer share ;
The Prince's flight, with trumpet call,
Sends me to battle from this hall.
False nephew! when we meet again,
'Twill be with host of armèd men,
And in the fight I will not pause
Till thou receive the victor's laws.
I hoped no more on my white hair
The burden of a helm to bear,
And thought to keep with thee at peace,
But thou hast made our concord cease.
In prayer I wrestled with the Lord,
That in the sheath might rest the sword ;
But thou hast drawn it by thy flight,
O perjured Prince ! and faithless knight."

Then Edward's brow grew dark as storm,
Again, like lightning, flash'd his eye,
And shook with rage his lofty form,
As thus he made reply :
" God grant that nothing may delay
The coming of decisive fray,
When deeds will with my words agree.
All kinship-ties away I throw,
I count my uncle as a foe ;

To strife I challenge thee !"
And on the ground he cast his glove,
And cried, " By all the Powers above,
Now swear to fight with me."
Montfort replied, " My sword and lance
Will never shun the battle's chance ;"
And with his blade he did prepare
To dash aside the swords of all
Who, in presumption proud, might dare
Dispute his passage down the hall.
And then he spoke to his brave son :
" Leave the false crew, come Henry, on ;
They who in friendship will converse
With one who hath scorn'd England's rights,
And is the falsest of all knights,
May draw upon their heads the curse
Which King, and Earl, and Prelate spoke,
Assembled in Red Rufus' Hall,
Letting their lighted tapers fall,
To be quench'd in foul stench and smoke,—
An awful curse, that should appal
Each one who hath the Charter broke."—
And on he strode, and none did dare
To lift against him weapon bare.

But Henry, ere he went away,
Soon to renew elsewhere the fray,
Turn'd to inquire with farewell glance
If Isabel had met mischance.
And, oh ! what sight his eye did see,—

It roused at once his jealousy.
The maid, with every grace adorn'd,
Who, oft and oft, his love had scorn'd,
To the strong arm of soldier clung,
A stripling, handsome, graceful, young;
Who, when the hall with tumult rung,
And every knight leapt from his seat
His foe with naked sword to meet,
Had courteously to help her sprung,
And tried her fear to calm ;
And bade her take his stalwart arm,
And he would lead her through the brawl,
Safe to her chamber, from the hall.

Young Montfort thought, " When swords did wave,
Would I had rush'd the fair to save.
This youth doth find what I did seek,
The hue of love is on her cheek ;
Would mine had been her helper's part !
I might at last have won her heart,
And been acknowledg'd as her knight,
To wear some favour in the fight,—
A silken scarf, or broider'd glove,
In token of the lady's love ;
But I must see this stranger win
The prize I for my heart design'd,
And now, before my eyes, begin
Himself into her love to wind.
The last of all my hopes is slain,
I do despair her heart to gain."

Such thoughts ran swiftly through his brain;
But when he heard his father call,
In accents stern, to leave the hall,
He cast upon the youth a look
That show'd he scarce the sight could brook,
And to rash purpose did incline,
To make him the sweet maid resign;
But reason quell'd his rising wrath,
And he drew not his weapon forth;
Grasping the pommel of his sword,
He follow'd his sire from the board,
Prepared the blows from him to ward.
But, from the moment that he spied
The sight that stirr'd his jealousy,
(Sign that her spouse he ne'er might might be,)
He sank into despondency,
And cared not if he lived or died.

Lord Cantelupe did not depart
Without unburdening his heart;
And frowning on the Prince,
Spoke thus, "I warn thee to take heed;
Barons, like those at Runnymede,
Are ready in their country's need
Their anger to evince.
Yea, thou shalt wish thy deed undone;
Remember thy grandsire King John,
Who aim'd to make himself too great
For English law,—think of his fate!"

Dame Maud no more restrain'd her wrath,
But knitting to a frown her brows,
At once in taunting words broke forth
Against her noble spouse.
" Is this thy vaunted loyalty,
To let the troubler of the realm,
Bad ruler of the nation's helm,
Go from our castle free?
Is ever glance of pity cast
On savage wolf, entrapp'd at last?
A traitor thou must be;
For trait'rous act it is, to spare
The tyrant caught within our snare."
The lord of Wigmore answer'd her:
" By blood of Christ, in Hales, I swear,
If the proud Earl fall on the field
In strife with me, as knight with knight—
(No otherwise with him I fight)—
His head to thee I yield;
That it may hang upon our tower,
For kites and ravens to devour."
The matron heard his oath with pride,
And in her heart her anger died.

Lord Genville knelt at Edward's feet
And said, " For pardon I intreat,
That I took Montfort's hest for law,
And ope'd to him my Castle door."
The gracious Prince gave him his hand,
And bade the loyal Baron stand;

And said, " I know that Leicester's order
Was back'd by an o'erwhelming host,
Or else thy fortress on the border
Had not to us been lost.
We all have quail'd before the Earl ;
But go with him upon his way,
And on thy keep, at dawn of day,
(For Leicester will no longer stay,)
My leopard-flag unfurl."
Lord Genville said, " Thy flag shall wave
On Dinan's tower, whate'er betide.—
I'll victory win, or find a grave,
Contending on thy side."

The lord of Dinan, ere he went,
To Wigmore's lady gave consent
His daughter should remain her guest.
The damsel gladly heard agreed
That she should not remount her steed,
But there that night take rest ;
For she with covert eyes survey'd
The grace in his young form display'd,
Who, 'mid the tumult, lent his aid ;
And knew not that the youth
Who now had ope'd her bosom's door
To thoughts she never own'd before,
Had pledged to one his truth,
Confirmed by many secret vows,
That he would take her for his spouse ;

And she, on whom his love was set,
Was her own friend,—fair Margaret.

Yes, Isabel, who never saw
In Henry Montfort aught to draw
Her love to him, began to see
In this young bud of chivalry
All that her fancy sought ;
His stature tall, and manly mould,
Frank countenance, and bearing bold,
Would well have graced a Court ;
She deem'd she never had beheld
One who in beauty so excell'd,
And answer'd to her thought ;
Nor ever in a shrine of flesh
A soul more simple, pure, and fresh ;—
So scarce her pleasure could contain
At the permission to remain
With him in Wigmore fort.

CANTO II.

WIGMORE CASTLE.

A S when the tempest's rage is o'er
The murmuring brooks their torrents pour,
So, now the angry strife had end,
A hundred babbling voices blend.
E'en ere the sound of Montfort's train,
Mounting their horses in the court,
Had died away, awoke again
The sound of mirth within the fort.
The hungry soldiers then did crowd
Round relics of the banquet proud;
And wit and humour circled free,
And cups were drain'd, 'mid laughter loud,
And all was joy and revelry.
Many were now the quips and jests
Passing between the jovial guests
About the " troubler of the realm,"
For so they Leicester styl'd :
The guider of the nation's helm,
Was in rude speech reviled.

Still Isabel turn'd glances soft
Upon her helper, Walter Croft,
The soldier who had caused a change

In all her former coldness strange—
For whom with love her bosom glow'd.
The Castle was the youth's abode;
For, when he was of tender age,
His father had been slain by foe,
And his fond mother, full of woe,
Ere to a convent she did go,
Had left him there, as page;—
But with his years ascending higher
The scale of rank, he now was squire,
Right courteous, prudent, sage;—
And fired with noble discontent,
To win renown his heart was bent;
And more, since Margaret he loved,
Was he to noble purpose moved.
In minstrel's lore he had been taught,
Was versed in arts of war and sport;
No one could better rule a steed
In tilt-yard, or on castle mead;
None was more ardent in the chase
Of all the beasts of savage race;
His arrow never missed the deer,
Woe to the boar that faced his spear!
When turn'd the grisly wolf at bay,
His lance was first the brute to slay.

The maid declar'd her wish to hear
The bold adventures of the day;
How Edward had sped safe away
From guards who sought his flight to stay.

And he told all in language clear;
But when he mention'd some mischance,
Threatening the fortune of his lance,
Pale hues o'erspread her countenance.
As summer sunshine ope's the rose,
His words her heart to him unclose;
A mood then came, before unthought,
The dream of love,—what joy it brought !—
In courteous tone Prince Edward ask'd
If Isabel would now be task'd
To make the company rejoice
With music and melodious voice.
She blush'd assent; a well-strung lyre
Young Walter, with attention bland,
Brought near, and set beneath her hand,
That it might sweep the wire.
In all the tones of music versed,
Her fingers struck a sweet prelude;
Her soft voice trembled at the first,
Then from her lips, in answer, burst
A song of merry mood.

"THE BALLAD OF FITZ WARINE.

" Fitz Warine carouses in Whittington Hall,
At the table feasts many a knight,
But a vassal his mind doth sadly recall
Who was wont to sit there on his right.

"The gallant Sir Andulf, who bravely fought,
Had in battle been overthrown;

And, by De Althiley, prisoner brought
To Pengwern's tower of stone.

"But Rampaigne, the harper, who loved his chief,
Observing his mien of sorrow,
Resolved to set free for his lord's relief
The captive, before the morrow.

"He dyed his red locks of the colour of jet,
His face of an ebon hue;
A soporous herb in his pouch he set,
And his harp he carried too.

"The sunset was painting the west with red,
When he gallopp'd o'er Rednall down;
The moon rose high over Wrekin's head,
As he came into Pengwern town.

"He strode up the hall where the Monarch quaff'd
Strong wine with De Althiley;
King John and his knights and barons laugh'd
The harper's dark face to see.

"He set down his harp and made it ring
With notes of music sweet,
To soothe the heart of earl, knight, and King,
And all who there did meet.

"Then out spoke the captain of Pengwern tower,
'To-morrow the head must fall

Of Sir Andulf, who spends a wearisome hour
While we are carousing in hall.

"'Oh! let his last eve be cheerful and gay,
Regaled with music and sport;
Let him hear this Ethiop wanderer play;'—
The Monarch applauded the thought.

"Unfetter'd he came, and De Rampaigne's wire
Thrill'd a note that the prisoner knew,
And hope in the captive's bosom did fire,
Unknown to the rest of the crew.

"King John conferr'd on the minstrel praise,
And bade him at once to bear
A flagon of wine, enwreath'd with bays,
To the company gather'd there.

"Now, quick! my good gleeman, drop into the cup
The well-pounded herb of power,
To seal all the wassailers' senses up
Save Sir Andulf's, for an hour.

"'Tis done; they quaff, and the harper calls
A soothing sound from the cord;
Ere long, the head of each guest falls
In slumber on the board.

"Then De Rampaigne hush'd his harmony,
And seized the poor captive's hand;

And whisper'd, 'At morn thou wer't doom'd to die,
But at morn thou free shalt stand.'

"They softly stepp'd over the rush-strewn floor,
Nor Monarch, nor liegeman stirr'd ;
The harper hath opened the studded door,
And the hinge no sleeper heard.

"Oh ! merry it was when Fitz Warine again
Beheld his guests in hall,
And a beaker of wine to the health did drain
Of Sir Andulf before them all."

To music light, with manner gay,
Sang Isabel her sprightly lay ;
And, when she ceas'd, threw glance around
Upon the laughing throng ;
And felt a gladness when she found
Young Walter prais'd the song.
"Of ballads I have heard with zest,
Lady, this lay of thine is best,
And minds us of the Prince's case,
Who lately led his guards a chase."
But Edward spake, in heart well pleas'd,
"Indeed, the song doth well accord
With this glad meeting round the board ;
But since our hunger is appeas'd,
And draught of wine hath sent the blood
To course our veins in swifter flood,
Say, would'st thou hear, my Lady Maud,

How I escaped from Hereford?
And, like Sir Andulf, am set free
From harsh restraint's monotony?"
Replied the dame, that nought so well
Would please her, as to hear him tell
The wild adventure of his flight,
That brought him to her home that night.

A silence reign'd throughout the hall,
And every eye the Prince did scan
When thus his story he began.
"A horse, the fleetest in his stall,
Sent by Sir Roger for my need,
Was led by groom to Widmarsh mead,
Beyond the city wall;
And there I rode on level ground
My guards' good horses round and round;
But when their glossy sides were wet,
With wreaths of foam, and steaming sweat,
I from the selle did bound,
And quick into the saddle vault
Of my led-courser, without fault,
In limb and breathing sound.
I scourg'd his loin, and spurr'd his flanks,
And, flinging brave De Ros my thanks
For courtesy I found,
My race for freedom was begun
On steed that could all steeds outrun;
Swifter than falcon toss'd from fist
Doth after flying partridge speed,

Swifter than swallow skims the mead,
Raced o'er the moor my gallant steed;
Behind his hoof uprose the reed,
As by light zephyr kiss'd."

" I heard a shaft whiz by my head,
From bow of archer truly sped;
My baffled guards came on my track,
Pursuing me as hungry pack
Of wolves chase deer through glade;
My horse still greater efforts made,
And bore me swiftly far away
From those who sought my flight to stay;
But, misconducted by a lane,
That winding round led back again,
I, in despair, drew up my rein,
Wond'ring where next to shape my course,
Or where to guide my willing horse;
But lo ! on hill of Lullington
A horseman on a charger grey
Was pointing out to me the way,
By signal I agreed upon.
He waved aloft a snow-white flag,
Directing me to Lady-crag.
Conceive, my friends, my great delight !
I never saw more welcome sight
Than when he waved this banner white.
The lord of Croft was that brave youth,
Before ye all I speak the sooth,
For his good deed reward should claim."—

Soon as the Prince pronounced his name,
All in the chamber loudly cheer'd,
And Isabel right glad appear'd.

The brave but modest soldier blush'd ;
And when the loud applause was hush'd,
The Prince resumed : " That pennon rais'd
Show'd me the way, and, God be prais'd !
Just as my savage guards drew near,
And almost touch'd me with the spear,
Just as I heard their coursers' feet
Close at my back the pebbles beat,
Arose behind a hill a shout,
And from their ambush started out
Sir Roger's men, with warlike gear,
Ready to stay my foes' career.
Sharply I spurr'd my charger's flanks,
And rode full speed into their ranks ;
Snatch'd a long spear from man-at-arms,
And, with my friends, faced round about ;
O ! then for me the strife had charms,
Of my success I had no doubt.

" With lance in rest, and heart aflame,
We met the foemen as they came ;
Two guards my lance hurl'd on the clay,
A score Sir Roger's men did slay,
The rest turn'd round and fled away.
They who had come like wolves, did flee
As yelping curs,—and I was free !

Thanks to thy husband and his squire,
And all their gallant company,
I gain'd my precious liberty!
I won my heart's desire!
But it were on my knighthood stain
If this brave youth a squire remain;
His deeds reward require."

"The lord of Croft, my helper bold,
Shall be among my knights enroll'd;
Though, to receive investure right,
His armour he should watch to-night,
He fought so well in my defence
I with that custom will dispense;
And now invoke her gentle aid
Who lately sang the merry song,
This eve, when he a knight is made.
To thee, fair lady, doth belong
To fasten, with thy fingers chaste,
The spur to heel, the belt round waist."
"Thy honour'd hest shall be obey'd,"
Lord Genville's daughter, smiling, said.

Prince Edward now with look gave sign
To monk, who sang for those who dine
On beef, and fowl, and venison,
The holy grace and benison.
The burly friar drew near the board,
Receiv'd from Walter Croft his steel,
And hallow'd it, and then restor'd

The weapon, with this grave appeal :
" Ever, with true and honest heart,
Through life take up the better part ;
Unsheath this brand in the defence
Of woman's right and innocence ;
And thus thy chivalry reveal.
Let it be terror to the strong,
Who do the weak and helpless wrong ;
Let it ne'er seek thy selfish gain,
But righteous cause alone maintain."

These earnest words, to honour dear,
From Isabel drew forth a tear ;
And when was heard his firm, " I will
Promise that duty to fulfil,"
She thought, " If he maintain the vow
Which solemnly he taketh now,
He merits well my hand and heart ;
But I must now perform my part ;"
So, from her seat of honour rose,
And while her visage scarlet glows,
Trembling, received from Mortimer
The broider'd belt and gilded spur ;
And, winning smiles of favour, went
To the young soldier, kneeling down
Before the heir of England's crown,
With forehead humbly bent.

The beating of her heart she heard,
And oft her quiv'ring fingers err'd,

Ere she had fasten'd on his heel
The pointed prong of gilded steel,
And, all in mind confus'd, had graced
With broider'd belt his manly waist ;
She trembled so, the silver clasp
'Twas long ere she had power to hasp ;
And glad she was when she had placed
The hallow'd sword in battle tried
Safe in the baldrick by his side.
Then o'er her eyes came such a mist ;
Unmark'd by her, Prince Edward's blade,
On Walter's shoulder softly laid,
Gave him the envied accolade,
And placed him on the honour'd list.
Sir Walter Croft unbent his knee,
And rose, the ceremony over,
And Isabel strove to recover
Her wonted calm complacency ;
But peace abides not with a lover.
The brave Prince then raised gaily up,
From the oak-board, a golden cup,
Fill'd with the juice of Loire's dark grape,
And pledg'd the health of the young guide
Who helped him to escape ;
And, while sweet Isabel he eyed,
He wish'd him, too, a virtuous bride,
Of lovely face and shape.
Then to his hardy knights did say,
" Be ready for a glorious fray,
That shall take all our shame away.

Soon beacons lit on many a height
Will tell the country of my flight;
The spectacle of scrolls of fire
Ascending from each mountain pyre
Will bring my gallant vassalage
Around me on war's bloody stage,
And my soul will a body find
Obedient to my daring mind;
Ere the green corn wear golden hue
Decisive battle will ensue.

" Banish the fear lest we may meet
Again with panic and defeat;
The Earl on Heaven his hope doth anchor;
But was not Bishop Acqua Blanca
Torn by his minions from the shrine
Of Ethelbert, at mass divine?
Judge, my good knights, will that commend
To Heaven De Montfort's cause?
No; God our struggle will befriend
With them who break His laws:
That deed of shameless sacrilege
Will sharper make my falchion's edge.
Or, see again his impious pride;—
Refus'd not Leicester to abide
By what King Louis did decide?
Yea, after he had sworn to take
For rule whate'er that Sovereign spake.
Companions brave! the victory's ours,
If righteous are the Heavenly Powers.

E

"Saxon and Norman aid I claim,
For Edward is a Saxon name
Deriv'd from the Confessor good,
And in my pulse beats Rollo's blood;
I will not shame the Norman brood,
But win a greater glory yet
To grace our line Plantagenet.
A blot imbues my royal shield,—
Our sad defeat on Lewes' field;
But blow of sword, and push of lance,
Shall win back my inheritance,
And set my father on a throne
Which will the nation's reverence own."

When thus his speech the Prince did close,
Shouts of applause around him rose;
The soldiers' voices shook the hall,
"To arms! to arms! we win or fall,
And rebel blow our spears will ward."
Some waved the cap, some waved the sword,
All vow'd to conquer with their lord.
Delight beam'd in Prince Edward's eyes
As round him rose those loyal cries;
But knowing they had need of rest,
He thus his trusty friends address'd:
"To-morrow will the breezes sweep
My standard, set on Wigmore's keep,
To show that I am bound for war;
The morrow will bring work for all,
Many will gather at my call,

My father's freedom to restore.
But now we gentle sleep require;"—
And, marshall'd by the seneschal,
The guests did from the hall retire,
And each laid down a weary head
In welcome slumber on his bed.

But while the tired warriors slept,
From hill to hill the bale-fires leapt,
And Edward's flight did wide proclaim
In characters of ruby flame.
The fiery race began from Clee,
Whence Shropshire heard the Prince was free;
Old Wrekin caught the gladsome news,
Nor passage of it did refuse;
The fire on Bardon summit spoke,
And Ingleborough Yorkshire woke;
Helvellyn summon'd Cumberland
To send to Edward's help a band:
So pass'd the tidings to the North,
Where pens and fells in flame broke forth.
And in the South, down after down
Assumed by night a fiery crown:
Malvern, with flame-like finger gory,
Points to May Hill the startling story;
And the round Mount a light displays,
That soon set Dunkery's top ablaze;
And Dartmoor told all Devonshire
That Edward did her help require.

So through the night the beacons blaz'd
News that the Prince's flag was rais'd.

But Isabel no sleep enjoy'd,
For thought how she had been employ'd.
She saw the youthful warrior kneel
Before her, arm'd in links of steel,
And honour'd badge of knighthood gain ;
So sleep forsook her fever'd brain.
She rose, the casement did unlatch
And open, and there stood to watch
The distant beacons' ruddy glare,
Across the sky of midnight, flare ;
And mark'd amid the stars appear
A comet, shap'd like fiery spear ;
This might have caused her heart to fear,
But softer feelings stirr'd her breast,—
Her thoughts did still on Walter rest.
He who had power her soul to move,
Might feel himself a mutual love ;
So, when endued with this surmise,
She knew how sweet are love's first sighs.

Now, wearied with her long day's chase,
She sought again her resting place ;
But, even while the maiden slept,
Memory of Walter still she kept.
And then for very joy she woke,
And found the morn o'er Clee had broke ;

Arose, and saw from valleys green,
Shelter'd the heathy hills between,
Sir Roger's vassals thronging in,
With horn and clarion's martial din;
And riding at each squadron's head,—
By Mortimer soon to be led,—
Came many a gallant border chief,
Who by his falchion won his fief,
And held it, by the same strong right,
Against the Welsh in stubborn fight.
But to her breast came no content
Until she reach'd the battlement,
And o'er the stony rampart leant;
And spied on tilt-yard turf below
Walter amid the squadrons go;
And heard his voice in loud command,
Bidding the horsemen wheel, or stand.

But deeper was her heart's delight
When peaceful hour of eve restor'd,
After his task, the youthful knight,
To meet her at the social board;
And the old seneschal assign'd
His place beside her when they dined.
Oh! how she then in rapture hung
On the sweet cadence of his tongue,
As he the name and style declared
Of warriors, who great deeds had dared.
Had Henry Montfort seen her *then*,
He had not known the maid again!

Pass'd in such sort ten days of May,—
How swift for her they fled away!
Too sweet, such joys, for long to last,
They soon were number'd with the past.

Oh! now no more her lovely face
Seem'd cold, and calm, and passionless;
In her flush'd cheek and kindling eye
Walter beheld love's tyranny.
He could not be insensible
To the great charms of Isabel,
Nor mark, unmov'd, her cheek assume,
When eye met eye, love's crimson bloom;
But mindful of his pledges given
To Margaret, in sight of Heaven,
He would not yield the maiden scope
To cherish in her heart a hope
That other purpose he design'd
Than to be courteous, gay, and kind.
Thought Isabel, " Sure it must be
Some lady holds his heart in fee;"
So hope and fear disturb'd her mind;
One hour she saw, the next was blind,
To indications clear and plain
That he wore love's soft flowery chain.

But sorrow o'er her did prevail;
She could not see, and not turn pale,
The armourer mending coat of mail;
Or the red glowing rim of steel

Press'd on the charger's hissing heel ;
Nor guildman, skill'd in bowyer's craft,
Shaping and fledging yeoman's shaft ;
Nor sword on sparkling wheel grow keen ;—
For all portend the battle scene,
And that Sir Walter must depart
And leave her with her sorrowing heart.
Nor to the depth of her fond mind
Was this despondency confin'd ;
It peep'd forth from her soul's recess,
And shadow'd all her beauteousness.
And often, when her friend sate by,
She turned away her glistening eye,
And from her bosom heav'd a sigh,
As if she hoped the deep-fetch'd sound
Would tell him of her secret wound.

But now at length the morning dawn'd
Of which her soul, foreboding, warn'd,—
The dark day, fated to bereave
Her heart of joy she doth receive
In converse with him, every eve.
Ere the sun rose, arose the maid,
In a rich robe her form array'd,
And did with pearls her tresses braid ;
Then went, and stood beneath the arch
Through which the horsemen soon must march.
When Walter to the gateway came,
She deemed it was a deed of shame
To tell what feelings in her burn ;

So only said, " On thy return
I hope to meet thee here again,
For in the Castle I remain."
Sir Walter heard, and thought to say,
" But I have given my love away,"
Yet this might drive her to despair,
So he did not the truth declare ;
But answer'd, " Soon may I receive
Welcome from those whom here I leave."
Her face then wore the brightest smile
That ever maiden's visage deck'd,
And Margaret he forgot awhile,
But soon the rising passion check'd ;
Yet clasp'd fair Isabel's white hand,
And wrung it with a warm adieu,
Mounted his steed that near did stand,
And rode the sombre archway through.

" I should have told him how I loved ;
That, though he doth from me depart,
He carries with him all my heart ; "
And after him her footsteps mov'd,
But soon were stay'd ; she must not ask
Of him delay from war's grim task ;
So turn'd, ascended to the tower,
And from the window of her bower
Caught the last glimmer of his lance
On which the early sunbeams glance
As he rode o'er a wooded bank ;
Heard the last clatter of the hoof

That bore him from her sight aloof,
And left her life a blank.
" Ah ! gone is now my gallant knight,
And gone with him my heart's delight.
A thought of love came not to me
Ere I his noble brow did see."
Now lake, and stream, and hill, look'd dark,
Her eye could not their beauty mark ;
The Castle seem'd a pile of stone,
And nothing more,—now he was gone !

But Isabel in her sad state
Was not completely desolate ;
Her fancy blent him with the scene
Of every spot where he had been ;
Her memory all his movements kept ;
She bless'd the ground where he had stepp'd.
When minstrels on their harps did play
She heard a music far away,
The echo of his martial lay ;
And turned her face and wept.
The words he spoke, the acts he did,
Were never long from memory hid.
So she, who once defied its strength,
Was vanquish'd quite, by love, at length.

CANTO III.

THE CONVENT OF LYMBROKE.

TWO summer months had danced along,
  Waking the flowers with sylvan song,
While Isabel at Wigmore stay'd,
Rejoicing in the faithful aid
Sir Walter gave the Prince's cause,
And that he won from him applause.
Yes, May hath glided into June;
The roses on the hedgerow spray
Have bloom'd, and faded all away,
The nightingale hath hush'd her tune;
June to July hath given way;
July to August's fervid ray;
The foxglove in the border-dells
Uprear'd her pyramid of bells,
Flourish'd amid the flowers a queen,
Then vanish'd from the woodland scene;
And monks of Wigmore view with pleasure
Their furrows bear the harvest treasure
On fields bestow'd by good Sir Hugh,
For whom they sing their masses due.
Yet Isabel remain'd
In Wigmore's fort indulging hope,

And striving with her fear to cope,
For hope she entertain'd,
That if Prince Edward won the day,
Contending in decisive fray,
And Walter lived and won repute,
He would return and urge his suit,
And ask her hand, which 'twas well known
To him that he could make his own.

While nature thus her work renew'd,
Meantime the unhappy nation view'd
The trouble of the Barons' feud.
For Edward, in the Monarch's name,
And Montfort, making equal claim,
From cottage, grange, and hall did draw
The best and noblest for the war.
And peasants' hearts with grief were torn
To see, by their own bullocks drawn
To either camp, their store.
Prince Edward's engines batter'd down
The ramparts of full many a town ;
His host did Gloucester's wall surround,
And entrance by a traitor found ;
Brecon and Worcester both were won,
And held for him by garrison.

Bristowe, the queen of all the west,
To Edward fealty express'd,
And from her richly laden quay
Sent up the Severn's watery way

Provision for the well-arm'd ranks
Encamp'd upon that river's banks.
In Hereford's rich shire reign'd
De Montfort, and his host maintain'd ;
But hoped by bridge of boats to cross
The Severn with his foot and horse,
And join his son young Simon's force,
And both together take the field
Against the Prince, and make him yield.

Meanwhile, in weary fights and frays,
Sir Walter won of all men praise,
And was the theme of minstrel lays ;
And all the border-country rung
With the renown of one so young ;
And Isabel, from many a tongue,
With joy heard of his gallant deeds,
How well in war his troop he leads.
And often on the wings of fame
To Margaret the story came
How brave was her adopted knight,
And in her heart she felt delight.
She went to walk for many an hour
Upon the rampart of a tower
Commanding distant view of way
Where first would come news of the fray.

Two summer months have sped along
In bloom, and beauty, and in song,
Since Dinan's hunters rode away

To rouse the wolf in Downton glen,
And Margaret chose behind to stay.
Lord Genville gone, and all his men,
To war, save those with hoary hair,
And limbs too weak the mail to bear.
She still remain'd.—Her daily prayer
Was that the sword might Walter spare ;
And oft at night she rais'd her eye,
Brimming with tears, toward the sky,
And trembled at the fiery spear,
Which look'd more large, more red, more near ;
To her it seem'd as if rush'd forth
An angel, with a scowl of wrath,
His hair blown backward by the wind ;
And so to fear her soul inclined.

One day, when August's sun rode high
In the clear fields of azure sky,
And no swift messenger had brought
Expected tidings from the host,
She left the tower, her wonted post,
And came into the grass-grown court ;
And bade a page to fetch her steed,
Mounted, and rode across the mead ;
Pass'd o'er the Teme in troubled mood,
And enter'd Whitcliffe's shady wood.

Oh ! what sharp pangs her soul did stir
When thoughts of Walter came to her ;

She noticed not the woodbine wreath
Climbing the oak, send fragrant breath ;
Nor tiny nut with fringèd sheath,
That peeped among the hazel-leaves ;
Nor the blue hare-bell she perceives,
That hung on stalk so frail and slight,
It quiver'd with the breezes light.
She rode along the green path, dreaming
That Walter's love was but in seeming ;
And, sometimes, wrapp'd in deeper gloom,
Him as unfaithful would assume.
O jealousy ! thou cruel lord,
Familiar at love's banquet-board,
Why didst thou rack her heart with fear
That Walter held her love less dear,
And Isabel, so full of grace,
Had, with dark eye and peerless face,
Shaken his constancy ?
" I wish I had been in her place
To set the falchion by his thigh,
And round his waist the belt to brace,"
She said, with heavy sigh.

Full of such gloomy thoughts she stray'd
To Deerfold forest's birchen-shade,
And her return to home delay'd
Till the broad sun began to glow
Above Mellenyth's purple brow,
And through the glade she and her horse
Cast giant shadows on the gorse,

And bee, with booty of the flower,
Flew humming toward her straw-built bower ;
Then thought to take the nearest road
Back to strong Dinan's safe abode,
But found it not ; perhaps a cry
May bring some woodman passing by,
To serve her as a guide.
So, like the tender bleat of lamb,
Calling on desert moor its dam,
She for some helper cried ;
And sylvan-echo, many tongued,
The sound of her weak tones prolong'd,—
No human voice replied.

Returning silence caused her fright ;
She saw a doe stamp on the lawn,
Then bound away to seek her fawn,
Safe shelter'd for the coming night,
And Margaret wish'd her home as near
As was its haunt to that poor deer ;
So rode on till her palfrey stood
On verge of hill, and through the wood
She saw, hugged close by hills around,
Below her lying, bright with flowers,
And broider'd with green hazel bowers,
A plot of meadow ground,
Through which a little purling stream
Did here and there in sunlight gleam,
But oftener hid, would wind and turn
Amid a paradise of fern.

The sun sank low behind the hill,
And all the air around was still,
Except where murmuring ran the rill ;
The scene appear'd so calm and blest,
That angels from the golden west
Might be descending there to rest.
But lo ! above yon rugged oak,
That rears aloft a wide-branch'd head,
With rosy gleam of sunset red,
Ascends a wreath of smoke.
" So, there are dwellers in the glen ;
They may be booty-seeking men
Who here have pitch'd their tent, and lay
Ambush for those who pass this way.
But hark ! what is that lovely strain
Breaking the stillness of the vale ?
It dies away, then swells again
With the soft breathing gale.
Is it a seraph in the wood,
That pours of melody a flood ?
No ! many voices have combined
To breathe that sweetness on the wind ;
And doubtless here, from tumult banish'd,
And living holy lives in God,
Some nuns have set up their abode ; "
So thought she, and her terror vanish'd.

The sunset tinged the heaven half through
With streaks and breadths of roseate hue
As down the gorsy hill she rode,

Until the peaceful valley show'd
A convent, and a chapel, where
Had issued forth the tuneful prayer
So sweetly on the evening air.
They made of grandeur no pretence ;—
The range of building round a court
Was built of stone, in rugged sort;
The little chapel form'd one side,
Exhibiting no mark of pride ;
Its windows own'd no tracery rich,
But, o'er the doorway, in a niche,
The Virgin's form she spied.
She rode on, and approach'd more near,
Halted, and heard distinct and clear,
Emerging from the cloister'd fane,
In low sweet tones, this vesper strain.

" Ave Mary ! mother mild,
Gentle nurse of sinless Child,
Listen while we chant our hymn
'Mid the forest-shadows dim.

" Ave Mary ! Virgin blest,
Watch beside our couch of rest,
And when morn reclimbs the skies
May we pure and holy rise.

" Ave Mary ! night falls fast,—
If its dark shade be our last,
Dawn our pole-star o'er the gloom,
Shine our beacon in the tomb."

F

"How sweet," thought she, "where birds sing praise,
And the stream chants an undersong
To their soft warbling all day long,
To hear these nuns their voices raise;
To hear them, gentle, good, and chaste,
Hymning amid the woodland waste."

The sun had set, the dew did fall,
When Margaret reach'd the Abbey wall,
And stay'd her palfrey near a door
Where the good nuns, with generous soul,
Gladly dispens'd a daily dole
Among their Saviour's friends, the poor.
The barrier reverently she eyed,
Where never suppliant was denied;
Knock'd gently, nor had long to wait
Before she heard, on stone-paved path,
Within the cloister round the garth,
Light footsteps hastening to the gate;
And saw in it an oaken slide
Drawn back, and face of one who spied,
And heard a voice in accents sweet
Say, "Who hath hither turn'd her feet?"
She answer'd, "One whose way is lost."
The hinges creak'd upon the post,
The door swung back; in white array
A nun appear'd, and thus did say:
"Welcome thou roamer with the deer;
We lately heard thy feeble cry,
And for thy safety felt a fear,

Lest harm to thee be nigh.
If thou had'st shouted in the night,
We from our tower had shown a light
To guide thee to our house aright.
This war the country doth disturb,
And men do deeds of villany
Which laws are powerless to curb;
So we are glad to welcome thee.
Enter our door, like weary bee
At eve returning to the hive,
And rest within our nunnery
Till morn the night away shall drive."

Then Margaret lighted from her steed,
Which an old man to stall did lead,
And follow'd through the door her guide
Around the cloisters of the square
To oriel-window'd chamber, where
The simple nuns their labour plied.
Stories of saints the walls illume
With varied colour; in that room
They prick'd the gold and silver thread
Into a cloth before them spread,
That when adorn'd with many a stitch
Would make their Chapel-altar rich.
But some depicted lily-flower,
And bird, and meek-eyed face of saint
On page of missal with their paint,—
So spent a blameless hour.

They rose up from their labour rare,
Duly perform'd with reverent care,
Bestow'd their greeting, helped to strip
Her mantle off, and press'd her lip
With welcome kisses warmly given,
As to a stranger sent by Heaven.
The board with pure white cloth they spread,
On it set cakes of oaten bread,
With savoury pasty of a doe,
Which good Sir Brian did bestow
On them whose hymns he lov'd to hear
When chasing through the wood the deer;
A flask of wine, distill'd from flowers
That bloom'd beside their holy bowers,
They added for her cheer.

When Margaret had her strength renew'd
With wine and venison's gen'rous food,
One of the pious maidens there,
The eldest of them, sister Clare,
Drew near to Margaret's seat her chair,
And said, " It gives us all distress
Our courteous lady Prioress
Cannot bestow on thee caress.
One sister in her company,
She left this morn our sanctuary ;—
May God avert from her all ill !—
She rode to where men fight and kill
Their fellow-men, and hopes to yield
Aid to the wounded on the field.

She said, ' A battle fierce drew nigh,
Or God would not set in the sky
The dreadful star, like to a spear,
Filling the hearts of all with fear ;'
And often asked herself, ' Shall I,
While brave men suffer, linger here ?
If I my help from them withdraw,
Surely I break my Saviour's law,
And I, His consecrated spouse,
Do not fulfil my holy vows.'
So she is to the armies gone ;
No doubt it gave her spirit pain
To face the wicked world again ;
But she, perchance, may meet her son,
Sir Walter Croft, the brave knight who
Serves with Prince Edward's valiant crew."

A thrill ran through the listener's frame
To hear the nun her lover name ;
And as she did the truth unfold,
Margaret remember'd Walter told
How his good mother went to dwell
A nun in Lymbroke's shady dell.
But Clare resumed : "We love the dame,
And miss her presence ; 'neath her smile
Our hearts shrink more from sin and guile.
But pardon if I talk too free,
For in this nook we seldom see
Any beside the poor we know,
And at a stranger's coming flow

Our words, belike, too rapidly.
My heart is for King Henry sore,
And of him I would fain hear more;
How fares he in the cruel war?"

"His heart," said Margaret, "must be cold
Who doth not for the Monarch feel,
Whom Montfort in his camp doth hold,
Waiting the turn of fortune's wheel.
Earl Leicester hath such power to rule,
The King is like a boy at school;
Subjected to his master-mind,
He must do all by him design'd.
The throne's indeed a thorny seat
To one for Abbot's chair more meet.
He sees the Barons' army thrive
And grow on his prerogative;
And harsh deeds, done by Leicester's hand,
Appear perform'd by his command.
The Chieftain leads him everywhere
He marches, but cannot deter
The King from spending wealth and pains
To help the monks in building fanes
At Worcester and at Westminster."

"'Tis well he gives," said sister Clare,
"His aid to raise those temples fair;
Worcester's new fane, I'm told, will be
A world of glorious imagery.
Like forest boughs that hide the skies

The arches of the nave will rise
On pillars, cluster'd like a sheaf,
And crown'd with sculptured flower and leaf.
Before the work commenced be done
Their earthly course will many have run."
But Margaret : " A Franciscan sage
Declares that in a future age
Still greater marvels will be wrought,
Far, far beyond the reach of thought ;
For men will walk beneath the sea,
And go without or sail, or oar,
In ships to ocean's further shore,
And bring down from the azure height
The moon and stars more near our sight."
But Clare said, " Sure no one receives
For truth what this mad monk believes ?
The wisdom of St. Francis spreads,
And still to greater progress leads ;
But how can future time unfold
Such things the crazy friar hath told ?
What ! will the world in which we stand
Become a kind of fairy-land ?
But tell me, for I wish to know,
More of the poor King, harass'd so."
Margaret replied, " Him I revere,
And more about him thou shalt hear.
He never passes any shrine
That he doth not a gift assign
In honour of the buried saint ;
Where Frideswide's holy bones are laid

And royal visit is forbade,
He there devotion duly paid,
In spite of priest's complaint.

"Arm'd with good conscience, he is bold,
But bears a heart of tender mould.
Once when in Blackmore's forest shade
He, with his hounds, pursued through glade
A milk-white and swift-footed stag,
And mark'd the fearful quarry flag,
And, panting, heave his furry coat;
He felt compassion,—blew a note
That called away the trackers staunch
Just as they reach'd the trembling haunch.
And when a knight, another day,
The lovely milk-white hart did slay,
A fine he made the hundred pay;
And every year is silver due
Because the knight the white hart slew."
So Margaret with the sister sate
Conversing till the hour grew late,
And in the sky the comet blaz'd,
That watchers everywhere amaz'd.
Then the kind nuns, with noiseless feet,
Did to their quiet cells retreat;
And she, conducted to a cell,
Found on a pallet-couch what spell
Hath travel long to woo to sleep,
And quickly sank in slumber deep.

The sun in robe of crimson rose,
And chased before his flashing eye
The mists that on the vale repose,
And deck'd the mead with jewelry;
The diamond's sheen could not surpass
The lustre of the dewy grass,
On which the feeding blackbirds run,—
Each blade seem'd like a litttle sun.
Early the cushat's amorous tone
Woke Margaret, in that convent lone,
And, when she woke, her glance did fall
On angels, painted on the wall,
That to her gentle spirit brought
Of heavenly happiness the thought.
The honeysuckle that entwined
The dodder'd oak its scent combin'd
With perfume of the wild-briar sweet
To woo her from her calm retreat.

She clad herself, and went to walk
In garden of the nunnery,
Where the good sisters loved to talk
Of Angels and Eternity.
But never nun walked there so fair!
The peaceful slumber of the night
Had made her countenance more bright;
Around her neck and bosom fair
Waved loose her locks of golden hair;
And, though she could not banish care,
As she inhaled the morning air

And slowly-paced where ripening pear
And apple on the branches hung,
And 'mid the leaves a radiance flung,
She seem'd a maid meet to entrance
Some youth with her fair form and glance.
But then the jealous thought return'd,
Born of the news which she had learn'd,
How Isabel was deep immersed
In love for him for whom she yearn'd,
And with her heart she thus convers'd.

"Would that some certain news might come
To strike the hateful rumour dumb
That Walter's thought doth rest on her
Who shares with me Lord Genville's care.
The dove that charms the leafy grove
With the sweet story of his love
Is true and loyal to his mate,
But mine forsakes me,—luckless fate !
I now know all the grief that tore
The gentle soul of young Llewellyn,
Who wooed me by the Mawddach's shore,
But cold indifference from me bore
While love was in his bosom dwelling.
But jealous thought I'll cast away,
And with these holy virgins stay ;
Let Walter wed with Isabel,
Who o'er his heart hath flung a spell
With shape and face surpassing mine,—
Let all his soul to her incline ;

I'll bear to him a sister's love,
Nor me shall stronger passion move ;
I'll love him as a sister ought,
And give to him no deeper thought.

" Here will I take a novice' vows,
And shroud with snowy veil my brows,
Where many bring their worldly wealth,
And find instead the soul's true health.
This valley, now with dew impearl'd,
Shall be to me my only world.
I have been haunted from my birth
With love of beauty of the earth,
And here I will enjoy the sight
Of that which brings the best delight ;
The joys of love, which are so sweet,
Hurry away on pinion fleet,
But there are pleasures that endure ;
Here, daily worship gently flings
O'er life the light of holy things,
And keeps the spirit pure."

Thus pondering deeply in her mind,
To be a novice she design'd ;
When, toward the convent, on white steed,
An armèd knight rode o'er the mead ;
On his lance-point the morning rays
Were twinkling in a starry blaze ;
A Cambrian robber, he may come

To plunder the poor sisters' home ;
See, now he is that oak beyond,
Where the stream broadens to a pond.
By terror seized, with footstep fleet
She toward the cloisters did retreat,
But, as she ran, turned round her neck
To mark if her fear-wingèd flight
Did the arm'd youth to chase invite ;
And she perceiv'd he sought to check
Her speed ; with lance his right hand waved,
As if an interview he craved.
The pennon that the spear-shaft show'd
Seem'd like the one her hand had sew'd ;
Her fingers rais'd the golden cloud
Of curls that her white brow enshroud
To fix on him a clearer gaze ;
A lock of hair his helm displays,
It is her tress she clipp'd and tied
On Walter's casque, when they had sworn
A love till death ;—it still is borne,
To mind him of his promised bride.
Yes, Walter Croft himself hath come
To see his mother in her home.

He halted near the thorny hedge,
Planted upon the garden's edge,
And o'er it did the maiden view,
And soon her lovely features knew ;
Down from the saddle lithely sprung,
The rein to bough of birch-tree hung,

Struck his long spear into the earth,
Amid the flowers that there had birth,
Unlatch'd and ope'd the wicket gate,
And lifting up his vizor's plate
He fondly gazed upon her face,
Then clasp'd her in a warm embrace.
Oh! where is now her pious mood?
Her wish to don a novice' hood?

"Why hast thou taken refuge here?"
Said Walter; "what had'st thou to fear?"
And then she told him of her ride
That led her here last eventide.
He spake, "Where is my mother, say?"
"The Lady Croft but yesterday
Rode forth, soon as arose the sun,
And with her went a pious nun,
To tend the wounded in some fray."
Then o'er his face there pass'd a shade,
As sadly he bespoke the maid.
"Alas! too swift the moments run,
And sterner duties must be done.
The Prince, at Worcester, will upbraid
If my march thither be delay'd;
Should the hosts meet, and I'm not there,
What load of shame will be my share.
Look, yonder on that mountain's verge
My gallant horsemen wave their spears,
And my return to lead them urge.
Nay, Margaret, restrain those tears."

"Thou gavest me to understand
Thy palm, now clasp'd within my hand,
Will shortly wield the battle brand;
And I perhaps may soon behold
My faithful Walter stiff and cold,
And have to kiss his spear or shield,
The only relics death will yield.
Can I hear this without a sigh,
And tear-drop moistening my eye?
Early I miss'd a mother's care,
Far from my mountain home I fare.
O Walter! I have only thee
To be my solace and my stay
In this wide world of misery,
And thou art hurrying hence away.
Oh! do not risk thy precious life!"
"With thee my honour is at strife,"
He said, "if thou should'st bid me shun
The loyal task I have begun."
"But stay," she said; "go not so soon;
Remain until the hour of noon."
"No, Margaret; where my honour lies
I must the call of love despise."

Then Margaret wiped away her tears,
And check'd awhile her choking fears,
And said, "Go forth in valour calm,
And may good angels nerve thine arm;
Let not thy spirit flag or faint
Till Edward turns the foe to flight,

And the King issues from restraint
Put on him by Earl Leicester's might,
And rules once more in Windsor tower,
And hath again a voice of power.
But, Walter, in the wild career
Of conquest, pity's pleading hear,
And as thy God may be thy Shield,
Be merciful to them who yield;
Follow the star of thine own soul,
And it will lead to glory's goal;—
And though 'tis sad to live alone,
I'll try to smile when thou art gone."

One more embrace and fervent kiss,
And sorrow follow'd after bliss;
For, from the spot with flowrets sweet,
He through the wicket did retreat,
And found again his steed,
Arching his neck down to his chest;
He mounted, and the spur impress'd,
And gallopp'd o'er the mead.
The gentle nuns, who had been brought
By neigh of his impatient horse
From out their cells to cloister-court,
Peer'd through the gateway, full of thought,
And their farewells did heed;
And when they saw those warm embraces,
They turn'd away with sadden'd faces;
For to their memories had come back
A sense of something they did lack,

But had conceiv'd in former days
Would, sometime, gladden life's sad ways.

The convent bell, with silvery tongue,
The nuns into the chapel rung,
And Margaret went with them to prayer,
And in the temple told her want
To God, in a sweet solemn chant,
And in their praise did share ;
When they had ended their appeal,
Departed with them from the choir,
And follow'd them to morning meal,
Which now she did desire ;
And while they satisfied their need,
One did a holy story read.
This o'er, spake Clare, with visage white,
And worn by vigil in the night,
" May thy young soldier prove more true
Than one who my affection drew ;
For I was once as fair and young
And warm of heart as thou art now,
And heard a youth, with flattering tongue,
To me a love undying vow,
But he did perjur'd traitor prove ;
I gave, but gain'd not, lasting love.
May thy betrothèd be more true,
And may'st thou never have to rue
His heartless act, and broken vows ;—
But if he choose another spouse,

Bring hither thy untarnish'd soul
Beneath our convent's calm control.

The Prioress will be thy friend,
And to thy slightest wish attend.
An endless sorrow clouds her brow
For loss of child, who would be now,
Were she alive, just of thy age;
In vain we try her woe t' assuage.
The memory of her babe endears
To her each maiden of thy years.
Her grief she vainly strives to hide
From us, who to the world have died.
The forest-dell she oft will seek,
And there for her lost offspring yearn,
And we behold, on her return,
The stain of weeping on her cheek.
Her cell we call the cell of tears,
The listener then her sorrow hears."
"How gladly would I give relief,"
Said Margaret, "to her constant grief;
But tell me how her child she lost,
And her life's happiness was cross'd."

"A score of summers have matured
Our harvests since a roving band
Of Welshmen scour'd our border-land,
And plunder rich secured.
Croft Fort was enter'd by the brood
Of robbers, and, steep'd in his blood,

Her husband lay beside his hearth;
The castle perish'd in a blaze;
And so began the mournful days
That cast a shadow o'er her path.
Her babe,—left with a guardian true,
While at her faithful vassals' head
She to the unequal contest flew,—
She saw no more, alive or dead.

" She search'd the ruin-cover'd ground,
And all the border-country round,
But her dear child she never found;
So rose an image in her brain,
Her daughter did on earth remain.
The thought within her mind is fix'd,
With every mood and feeling mix'd.
If at some shrine were bent her knees,
It would her warm devotion freeze;
While sitting at a social meal
Over her memory it would steal,
And make her food forbear;
Whate'er she suffer'd or enjoy'd,
Howe'er her time might be employ'd,
She only thought of her.
Eight years she spent in hope like this,—
A hope that bloom'd not into bliss;
But oft found solace when she stood
In meekness near the holy Rood,
Learning thereby to bear her loss
By weighing it with Christ's own Cross,

And trusting vainly that she might
Regain the child she lost that night ;
At length she sought out convent lowly,
And gave herself to worship wholly ;
But still the flattering hopes remain,
And oft she dreams her child to strain
To her fond breast—then wakes to pain.

"Come, spend with us thy womanhood
In prayer and praise and doing good.
Dear friend, our hours are never dull,
But of a rich enjoyment full ;
Beside the bliss of daily prayer
We many a simple pleasure share.
By art we labour to express
Our yearning after loveliness ;
Pictures of all fair things we draw,
And colour with the brightest hue
Of gold, green, red, and heavenly blue,
Around the margin of the page
That tells us of another age,
Make us to prize our volumes more.
We love to watch the little birds
That round our tuneful chapel throng ;
They seem to comprehend our words,
And listen to our song.
The linnet from the ravenous hawk
Finds refuge with us as we walk ;
The conies and the hares appear
To feel at us no pang of fear,

But only halt, and prick the ear ;
The stags look with large hazel eyes,
But soon abandon their surprise ;
Our forms, clad in our garments white,
To bird and beast are welcome sight.
We give to every plant a name
Of some good saint our love doth claim ;
And pious name we give to places
That God with special beauty graces.
We mark the joy it gives the poor
To see us at their cottage door.
Oh ! come, partake with us the treasure
Of many a pure and guileless pleasure."

But Margaret said, " Not to my mind
Are now joys of transcendent kind ;
Your days of worldliness are pass'd,
Your lot is with the angels cast ;
But I look for some happy days
With him whose love my heart doth praise
Ere I tread death's dark downward ways.
Time in the tomb is very long,
And life is short, e'en to the strong,
And now to me seems very bright
With promise of a rich delight ;
But if sad fate my bliss shall blight
I from the world will here retire,
As from a fatal raging fire."

Then sister Clare rais'd up her veil,
And bared her cheek, with fasting pale ;

And Margaret kiss'd her gentle face,
And did the other nuns embrace,
And said, " I will return to home,
From whence I yesterday did roam."
Then sister Clare once more spake thus :
" Oh ! rather stay ; be one of us
While thou art free from fleshly stain,
In our pure happy home remain."
Margaret replied, " Not now, not now
Will I pronounce the holy vow ;
But something whispers in my heart
That I of shame shall feel the smart,
And hither come, not to depart."
" I'll pray," said Clare, " both day and night
That thou may'st share our pure delight."

CANTO IV.

THE MARCH.

WALTER, meanwhile, for battle bound,
　　Led on his troop of men in mail
Through Deerfold's hilly forest-ground
Into Teme's fertile vale.
The great renown which he had won
Drew to his band the lords of Clun ;
Hopton and Lingen's gallant knights
(Foremost in furious border-fights)
Rode also, 'neath his flag, that bore
On azure field a lion d'or.
The troop, o'er which that flag he rears,
Number'd more than two hundred spears.
Since he must Worcester reach that eve,
Nor Edward in great peril leave,
He urged his men to mend their pace,
And gladly they did onward race.
From Richard's fort the noontide hour
Pealed as they rode by Cornwall's tower ;
The steers, knee-deep in herbage, cast
A lazy look as on they pass'd.
Some Welsh had march'd to left of Teme,
So *they* cross'd by a bridge that stream,

And soon their horses' speedy feet
Struck fire from Tenbury's stony street.
From Hanley's upland swains could see
The crimson pennons waving free.

Their way then left the breezy height,
And they rode down a shady lane,
Through soil that bore a ruddy stain,
And saw a cliff, abrupt and white,
Between the hill and meadow ground
Rise, with a little chapel crown'd.
The fane was sacred to St. John ;
And, in a cave below, did won
A hermit, who for sin made moan,
And penance suffer'd all alone ;
And, deeply studying in his cell,
Signs of the future time did spell.
As lower down the horsemen rode,
They spied the entrance of a cave,
O'er which the ivy-tresses wave,
And a small stream that near it flow'd
Over the cliff the lime had made
Fell in a foaming white cascade.

High on the rock, rugged and hoar,
Near to the modest chapel door,
In russet garb, stood the recluse
Who did the cave for dwelling choose ;
A twisted cord his brown robe braced

Loosely around his sunken waist ;
A long beard, white with snow of age,
Waved on the bosom of the sage.
On the rock's verge beside him stood,
Rough carv'd in oak, the holy Rood ;
To this he pointed with his arm ;
A wild light sparkled in his eye ;
In strange shrill tone that brought alarm
He warn'd the passers by.

"Ye go in battle to engage
Where Christians war with Christians wage ;
The Holy Cause doth suffer loss.
The hill where Christ hung on the Cross,
The cave where He lay in the tomb,
Are by the Moslem still possess'd ;
All Christendom should be in gloom,
Nor any other warfare press'd
Save that against the Paynimry,
Who will not leave a passage free
For pious pilgrims to repair
And kneel in humble worship there.
Woe to the man who to that strife
Prefers or home, or land, or wife."
And then more shrill his accent rose :
"Who, shrinking from the great Crusade,
Fights with his own, and not God's foes,
On him a dreadful lot be laid !
God writes the future on the stars,
And they foretell much blood and scars.

I heard last night a dismal wail
Pass from the forest down the vale;
And saw at morn, fly to the east,
Dark ravens croaking for a feast."

So spake the monk; and Walter felt
The stern reproof his language dealt;
But then he thought of Margaret
And Isabel, whose prayer made friends
For him in Heaven, that o'er him bends.
He tried the menace to forget,
Yet deep it sunk into his heart,
Nor would from memory depart.
His comrades, too, with terror quail'd,
And silence through the troop prevail'd.
Soon from the rock they turn'd their steeds,
And took the way through Shelsley meads.
The moated fort of Ham was gain'd,
And there they food and wine obtain'd,
Their failing strength to cheer.
Then crossing Teme by rustic bridge,
Ascended the opposing ridge;
In sight, Twinberrow's hills appear.
Their steeds bore them with rapid hoofs,
Where Martley rais'd her straw-built roofs,
And soon they came to Severn-side,
And saw, upon the farther bank,
Fair Worcester rear her walls in pride;
Some strong monks there a ferry plied,
And many bore to Edward's rank.

They urged the boat the stream across,
And each man enter'd with his horse;
Then came to land beside a mound
On which a Norman Castle frown'd;
Upon the ramparts guards appear'd,
And seem'd at first of them afear'd;
But when they saw the troop display'd
The flags of those who Edward aid,
Their friends they loudly cheer'd.

The horsemen through the water-gate,
And close of Priory, rode straight;
And saw the skill'd Freemasons stand
On scaffolds round a half-built pile,
To be a new Cathedral plann'd,
And stone on stone with even hand
Lay firm, on walls of nave, and aisle,
And chancel, rais'd in Gothic style.
Around the fabric workmen toil,
Squaring the blocks, the quarry's spoil,
Or hewing, with repeated stroke,
Huge rafters from the solid oak
Of trees that lately did aspire
In woods of Feckenham and of Wyre.
Near to the building stood the cranes,
Each with a strong arm, that sustains
The swinging blocks, and lets them fall
Into the places in the wall.
And then the tinkling sound was heard
Of trowel that the mortar smear'd;

And grating noise of jagged saw,
Which the rude churls through sandstones draw;
And monks were near, their hearts aglow
With joy to see their temple grow,
And thinking the Cathedral fair
Would unto future times declare
How great the men of that age were.

The troop soon came into the street,
And down it rode, while burghers greet
With flags and 'kerchiefs that they wave
The arrival of the squadron brave.
The tents of Edward were array'd
On mead beyond the northern wall;
Pennons and flags on them display'd
Show'd some from every shire obey'd
The gallant Prince's call.
As through the canvas-town he rode
Walter remark'd each band's abode.
De Clare's red lion proudly ramp'd
On folds of standard where encamp'd,
From Gloucester's vale, a hardy crew,
Equipp'd with mighty bows of yew.
And soon he heard, not without pride,
(Where Mortimer his banner rear'd,)
The coming of the squadron cheer'd
By those with whom he oft did ride,
Chasing with hounds the antler'd stags
That bell'd on Deerfold's wooded crags;
Then, rode to war on small rough nags,

Which, picketed by Severn's edge,
Were champing now the watery sedge.

Prince Edward came his friends to meet,
And did their leader warmly greet.
" Receive, " he said, " our grateful thanks
For the brave troop led to our ranks.
We made a rapid march last night
To Kenilworth, and found our foes,
After a revel, did repose
Within the town ; they woke in fright.
Young Simon safely cross'd the lake ;
Others, half-clad, our men o'ertake.
A score of careless knights we caught,
And to our camp at Worcester brought ;
Their baggage and their horses seiz'd.
Our grooms and pages were well pleas'd ;
He who went there on sorry hack,
Rode on a splendid charger back.

" But Leicester means the die to cast
Of battle, and the Severn pass'd,
Hath pitch'd his camp in Kempsey park,
But he will raise it e'er the dark,
And straight to Evesham march anon,
In hopes to meet his rebel son.
Thy troop shall with my squadron ride
This evening by the Severn side
Northward some leagues, then wheel about,
And by short way to Evesham speed ;

Gloucester will march by other route,
And Mortimer, with stores we need,
Toward that town, where we shall meet,
And make our solemn last appeal,
By the decision of the steel,
And Montfort's host, I trust, defeat."

But now I will Sir Walter leave
To rest until the march at eve,
And say whom gentle Margaret
Upon her homeward journey met.
A trusty yeoman at her side,
She did through Haywood forest ride,
And came to hill call'd Mary-Knoll,
Whose sloping banks were to their tops
Clad by the oak and birchen copse,
And at whose feet a streamlet stole
A murmuring way through hazel bushes ;
In spring first carol there the thrushes ;
Here, first, the cooing stock-doves pair,
And earliest primrose blossoms fair.
The beauty lured her from her selle
To wander down toward the dell,
And, in that Eden of the grove,
Indulge in happy thoughts of love.
Here Walter dragg'd the clusters hung
On hazels high, beside the brook,
Down to her reach, with ashen crook ;
Or clomb the loftier tree, and flung
The nuts, which autumn suns embrown,

Into the lap of her white gown,
While clear her laughter rung.

The yeoman, while the maiden strays,
Rested, and watch'd her palfrey graze,
And only mark'd where she might be
By the dove bursting from the tree.
Not long she sate beneath an oak,
When on her close retirement broke
A soldier, in mail armour clad,
Who in his hand a long lance had.
She look'd; Oh! did her eyes see true?
Did she her former lover view?—
Of stalwart shape, in bloom of age,
One who had tried her love to engage,
But vainly had employ'd his art
To win the favour of her heart.
She quickly sprung up from her seat;
Llewellyn knelt down at her feet,
And seiz'd and press'd her struggling hand
Against his lip, and then did stand,
Fixing a keenly piercing stare
On her blue eyes, and visage fair;
But in her lovely face and eyes
The same firm purpose he descries
That often had his suit denied,
While he sate trembling at her side.

On him she gazed, bashful and dumb,
While nought was heard but wild bees' hum,

Or murmur of the leaves and stream,
That lately wooed her mind to dream.
He spoke the first : " I see thine eyes
Bend on me look of wild surprise,
But from my lips thou now shalt learn
Why to thy presence I return.
Our Prince, Llewellyn, will espouse
De Montfort's daughter, Eleanor,
And, to confirm his ardent vows,
Hath sent his future sire-in-law
A martial force, some thousands strong ;
With them a lance I bore.
This morn they march'd this road along,
And, from a peasant whom I saw,
I learn'd,"—and here he heav'd a sigh,—
" What were my thoughts, no tongue can tell,—
That thy dear presence was so nigh ;
That thou in Dinan's fort didst dwell.
I long'd to see thee once again,
And press my suit, though 'twere in vain ;
And when from the old man I heard
Abroad thou wentest yesterday,
And homeward would'st return this way,
My further march deferr'd,
And rode into this wood to wait,
And hear thy lips decide my fate ;
For my love is as warm as ever,
And prompts me to one more endeavour.
O Margaret ! say but one kind word,
And my lost peace will be restored."

First pallor, then returning red,
Over her lovely features spread.
"To meet thy love I oft have striven,
But the same answer must be given;
A difference between us lies,
I cannot with thee sympathize;
No one to love can be compell'd."
Then jealousy his bosom swell'd.
"I see! I see! thou seekest one
Of richer fortune, higher rank;
But some deed may by me be done
For which my Prince, thy friend, will thank
And grace his vassal; so may I
Ascend in thy esteem more high."
"No grace of birth or rank I seek,
No store of wealth, I'm not so weak;
Though high thou risest in the scale
Of honour, thou wilt not prevail.
Forgive, forget, the fault in me,
That love I cannot bear to thee.
When in the sky doth mount the sun,
The reign of lesser lights is done;
The truth I cannot, must not smother,
My heart is given to another."

Three backward steps the youth did take,
As if he trode on venom'd snake;
And once or twice paced up and down;
At length he cleared away his frown,
Though tears stream'd from his eye.

" Destroy'd is all my earthly bliss ;
And thou hast been the cause of this."
But Margaret made reply :
" Gwynedd hath many blooming maids
Who sigh for love in hazel shades,
And fairer forms than mine possess ;
Woo one of them with fond caress,
And on thy courtship wait success !
Pluck up the plant that bears no fruit,
And set another in its stead
That will an autumn burden shed."
" Pluck up my fond heart by the root !"
The youth in trembling accents said,
" No, Margaret ; thou mistak'st my love ;
'Tis too deep-rooted to remove.
Oh ! if I love, I love for ever,
And naught my heart from thee can sever ;
Unless I wed thee, I remain
Unbound till death by nuptial chain."

His constancy the maid admired,
And one kind look her blue eye fired,
And with more warmth the youth inspired.
"Oh ! give me somewhat to recall,"
He said, " my hours in Bradwen's hall,
And by the Mawddach's rolling tide,
Where I my first devotion sigh'd ;
A token that thou dost not hate
One who would link with thine his fate."

H

A deeper blush her visage stain'd,
Her heart was by his trouble pain'd ;
She could not see his piteous look
And feel within her heart rebuke.
And she no more her soul could **harden** ;
So, **from** a posy cull'd in garden
Of Lymbroke's nunnery, forth drew
A **rose**bud of a crimson hue,
And at his feet the flow'ret dropp'd.
He to his lips the red bud press'd,
Then laid it near his heart to rest,
While deep emotion language stopp'd.
But power of speech once more he found,
And with it sought her heart to sound.
" Soon fields of battle will be spread
With **bodies of the youthful dead** ;
Oh ! if thy hand should e'er be free,
Say, Margaret, wilt thou think of me ? "
" Speak not again those cruel words,
Which hint that my betrothed **may die** ;
They pierce my heart like sharpen'd **swords.**"
So Margaret made reply.
But he, " Perhaps my own life-blood
May redder tinge this little bud,
And fatal stroke may send me where
I shall be freed from all despair."
The sound of sorrow **and of tears**
In his sad tone of voice appears ;
He turn'd, and quickly left the place,
Illumined by her beauteous face ;

And gain'd his steed, tied by the brook,
Mounted him, spurr'd, and overtook
And mingled with the well-arm'd band
The Prince had sent from Cambrian land.

CANTO V.

THE BATTLE OF EVESHAM.

PRINCE EDWARD'S tents at eventide
   Were struck, and all his host rode forth,
And Walter with them, toward the north,
Misleading scouts who them espied.
But when arose the round full moon,
And burnish'd with a silvery gleam
The playful ripple on the stream,
Their feignèd course was alter'd soon,
And the proud standards did invade
The depth of Feckenham forest's shade.
All night rode on the men of war
Among the trunks of oak-trees hoar,
And often mark'd through thicket peer
The branching antlers of the deer,
That, when the shining arms they saw,
Snuff'd at the gale, and toss'd the head,
And to more distant copsewood fled;
And oft was heard the surly swine,
Whetting his tusk against an oak;
And rush of herd of milk-white kine
That through the bushes broke.

But when more sparsely grew the trees,
And freshly blew the morning breeze,
And eastern sky was streak'd with light,
The army halted on a height;
From whence they saw some white tents gleam,
Beside a town and winding stream,
Before an Abbey grey,
That 'mid the valley's soft repose
Like to a lofty rock arose,
Awaiting dawn of day.
" Yonder," said Edward, " on that plain,
Stand Evesham Abbey, town, and fane,
And Montfort's tents spread their array;
But we will on that hill take post
That lies betwixt us and his host,
And bar his northward way."

Sir Walter said, " They may retire,
And not advance to face our ire;"
So Edward to Sir Walter spake,
And did a wise precaution take.
He bade his soldiers to bring forth
The flags they took at Kenilworth,
And raise them up before his van,
That Montfort might their blazon scan,
And knowing not they had been lost,
Conceive they waved before the host
Of his bold son, and not retreat,
But forward march the foe to meet.
And then he sent two hundred horse

The Avon at Cleeve ford to cross,
And keep in check young Simon's force
If on that bank he took his course.
And when the Prince all this had plann'd,
He gave his army the command,
Without or trump, or clarion blown,
To march from Lenches' summit down.
As foxes in the twilight grey
Stealing along to seize their prey
The host in silence downward went,
And at the end of the descent
Beheld upon the road, that round
The furzy slope of Craycombe wound,
The spears of Gloucester's army, thrust
Through a great moving cloud of dust.
The Prince then sent in haste a knight
To bid the Earl wheel round the height,
Where soon his own halt would be made,
And eastward lie in ambuscade ;
And when De Montfort moved his rank,
Make fierce assault upon his flank.

From Evesham's wall ascends the ground
Toward the north ; that hill was crown'd
By the false standards raised ;
And when the sun on Cleeve hill glow'd,
And all the golden valley show'd,
Their scrolls with lustre blaz'd.
Behind them, Edward's horsemen stood ;
Their spears rise up, as firs in wood.

Sir Walter look'd toward the tower
Whose bell invites the monks to pray,
And, on its top, saw watchman scour
With glances keen that war array ;
Trying to spy if in the rear
Unfriendly standards did appear.
He sees them ;—trumpets sound alarm,
And where the white tents stood arranged
The tranquil scene is soon all changed.
Soldiers rush forth in haste to arm ;
And as in spring, meads are alive
With bees that swarm out from their hive,
So men in mail pace to and fro,
Preparing to attack the foe ;
And into band and troop collect,
Each with its own proud banner deck'd.

But when they were drawn up in rank,
And ready to ascend the bank,
A solemn note the trumpet sent ;
Riders dismounted from the selle,
And prostrate near their horses fell,
And spears and halberds downward went
As to the soil the footmen bent.
Yeomen set down their unstrung bows,
And, with arms cross'd, lay on the ground ;
The same did every soldier round.
Now for awhile was heard no sound ;
At length, the solemn voice arose
Of Worcester's prelate, Cantelupe,

Who in white robe before them stood ;
And lifting up the blessed Rood,
Assoil'd each band and troop.
A cheerful note the trumpet blared,
And every warrior rose from earth ;
The horsemen tighten'd saddle girth,
And to remount prepared.

When to the saddles they had sprung,
And archers had their yew-bows strung,
The trumpets sounded,—bugles blew,—
And—sight magnificent to view !—
Straight up the hill the army steer'd,
To force a passage through their foes ;
And, like corn waved by wind, appear'd
The mass of spears that rose.
The horsemen rode on either wing,
In front the bowmen drew the string ;
And, as they up the hill did crowd,
The sky grew dark with inky cloud ;
The thunder rattled fierce and loud,
And lightning spread a fiery shroud,
And in red rapid flashes gleam'd,
That like the dart of angel seem'd.

'Mid the foot-rank, the Welsh allies
March'd sullen, with no battle-cries ;
" What matter where the victory lies ? "
They thought, " all are our enemies ;
We came to fight on Montfort's side,

Since Eleanor may be the bride
Of our young Prince.   Why should we stay?
We'll seek our hills and streams again."
And so they threw their spears away,
And fled, wide scatter'd o'er the plain;
But Margaret's Cambrian lover then,
Llewellyn, blamed his countrymen;
And, reckless of his own sad life,
To turn some few from flight prevailed,
And with De Montfort's army scaled
The hill, to face the strife.

From Montfort's archers, thick as snow,
Fell feather'd arrows on the foe;
Then Edward's bowmen bent the yew,
And brought the long dart to the head,
And loosed the cord; the keen shafts flew
Upon their errand dread.
And Leicester's horsemen from their steeds
Were thrown, their mail-pierced by the reeds;
His footmen, bleeding, struck the sod,
And o'er their limbs their comrades trod
In a confusion wild.
When many horses riderless
Ran snorting from the bloody press,
Prince Edward grimly smiled;
But, for a while, his knights restrain'd.
" Be patient till the height is gain'd;
A few more moments rest ye still,
And ye shall hurl them down the hill."—

Within ten lengths of horseman's lance
The fierce assailants made advance ;
Then Edward shook his spear and cried,
"Thou, Simon Montfort, art defied !
My gallant men ! upon them charge,
And drive them back to Avon's marge."

They gave their eager steeds the rein,
Each holding shield before his heart
And sloping spear beside the mane
They for the struggle start ;
But Montfort's horsemen struck the goad
In chargers' flank, and forward rode.
A dreadful sound smote on the ear,
When met the hosts in full career ;—
The thunder of the horses' tread,
The shivering of lance or shield,
The clash of sword on helmèd head,
Then sounded through the field.
The monks who in their temple pray'd
Heard the dread noise, and were dismay'd ;
The friar who watch'd from bell-tower,—all
The awful tumult did appal.
Death gleam'd upon the lance's point,
Which ruddy life-blood did anoint;
But when the spear broke on the foes
The fragment down was flung,—
The warrior in his stirrup rose,
Aloft his falchion swung ;
Or whirling round his battle axe,

Clove through the soldiers' mail like flax,
Or wielding mace with many a spike
Did on the iron helmet strike.

As when a mighty northern breeze
Blows and o'erturns the forest trees,
Before the shock of Edward's troop
The chargers fell upon their knees,
And many a helm did stoop ;—
Many a banner sank to ground,
And shrieks, and shouts, and yells resound.
Young Henry Montfort foremost came,
One gallant wing of horse he led,
And longed to win or death, or fame,
And so put Isabel to shame,
Who chose a lover in his stead ;
But struck by lance upon the breast,
And backward o'er the crupper press'd,
He fell to earth as dead.

No bolder deeds were done that day
Than by young Walter in the fray ;
The helm of Devereux he cleft,
And hurled him down of life bereft ;
Where'er he strong resistance met,
That only did his ardour whet ;
He hew'd a straight and yawning pass
Right through the army's stubborn mass.
Remembering what the hermit said,
He vow'd, when ended was the war,

To go with Edward on Crusade,
And so his snowy surcoat bore,
Over his heart, a ruddy Cross ;
And, mounted on a milk-white horse,
Appear'd,—amid the throng of men,—
As if St. George had come again !
And, like that Saint, he check'd his steel
If one for mercy did appeal.
When Henry Hastings' falchion broke
At once he stay'd his deadly stroke,
And offer'd him his own good brand,
That he might, arm'd, his axe withstand.
For Margaret's sake he sought for fame
And glory to adorn his name,
That when the holy marriage rite
Link'd it with hers, the union might
Bestow on her more true delight.

But, as he braved the foemen's wrath,
Llewellyn cross'd his dangerous path ;
The face of neither could be seen
Behind the vizor's iron screen.
Sir Walter charged with all his force,
And overthrew him and his horse ;
And as he lay upon the mead,
Bent o'er him from his stronger steed,
And shook his brand above his head,
And in his heat had struck him dead ;
But memory of Margaret's word,
Toward the vanquish'd to be kind,

Came o'er him, and he changed his mind.
Then lower'd down his blood-stain'd sword,
And cried, "For my dear lady's sake
Receive the life my steel might take."
The conquer'd warrior heav'd a sigh,
As if his spirit, full of gloom,
Could not within his breast find room;
And, moaning, made this sad reply:
"On earth I care not to remain,
To love, and not be lov'd again;
Come, thrust thy sword, and let me die."
Sir Walter felt a pang of ruth
For the despairing love-sick youth,
And bade a squire to search and bind
With lint his wounds, that bled apace;
Then turn'd, more vigorous foes to face.

He everywhere appear'd to seek
The strong t' oppose, but spare the weak.
As thus he strove, he spied a knight
Arm'd as Earl Leicester for the fight,
And like him in his lofty height;
Devices on his shield and coat
Him to be Montfort did denote,—
Behind the vizor's iron screen
The warrior's face could not be seen.
Sir Walter rais'd his sword for blow,
But Montath, Lord of Hawarden,
The leader of the Flintshire men,
Before him to the strife did go,

And with his falchion clove the clasp
That did the foeman's helmet hasp
To gorget,—and the casque fell down,
And show'd the head that wore the crown;
And from his lips these words did spring,
"Strike not again, Oh! spare thy King,
Henry of Winchester; I claim
Allegiance in my royal name."
Sir Walter to his bridle sped,
And seizing it, the Monarch led
Along a road his sword made clear,
Of living foes, but paved with slain,—
While Montath held the other rein,—
In safety to the rear.

The Prince's valour nerv'd his band;
He at their head to danger flew,
And gallantly fought hand to hand
With foes, and many slew.
"Courage! my comrades; if ye die,
Revered shall be your memory;
Fight manfully, and if ye live,
Honour and land I vow to give;
Fight fiercely, and ye fight no more,
This battle will conclude the war.
But rebel Montfort! thee I seek,
Vengeance upon thy head to wreak;
Oh! recollect thy solemn vow,
And face me in the conflict now."
Thus shouting, through the press he hew'd

A path with cloven limbs bestrew'd,
And when he sought the Earl in vain
Cut to his troop a road again;
And often breathing furious threat,
Montfort he sought, but never met.

So, on Prince Edward's side, the battle
Raged fiercely, while the thunders rattle
And roll along the clouded sky,
And icy showers of stones of hail
Tinkled against the warriors' mail.
At Montfort's angry menace, close
The gaps made in his rank by foes;
Where'er his friends most succour need
He gallop'd on his strong black steed,
That, while the rider smash'd the mail
As easily as shell of snail,
Would, with his horny hoof, crush down
Opponents, cracking rib and crown;
Or, blending blood with bridle froth,
Mangle the assailants with his mouth,
And those he tore with his sharp teeth
Would trample his hard feet beneath.
As some fierce Northman from the dead,
Wherever rush'd that giant dread
Upon his coal-black horse
The blood of noble hearts was shed,
And down sank many a corse.
No one he cast upon the plain
Ever remounted steed again;

And many only at the sight
Of his strange superhuman might
Grew pale, and shunn'd the deadly fight.

To flee his adversaries turn :
Their flight was seen by Bassingbourne ;
The dastards he upbraids :
" On Lewes'-plain is not the fray
We fight on Evesham-field to day ;
Again, again, ye renegades,
Will ye your cowardice display ? "
Nor less Sir Walter's efforts brave
A courage to the caitiffs gave :
" May I my charger ride no more
If this long lance drink not your gore,
For ye disgrace again your shield."
So the two knights to them appeal'd,
And brought them back into the field
To struggle with the foe.
And valour, feebleness replaced ;
Those who had fled, now others chased,
And answer'd blow with blow.

And now the one side did prevail,
Now fortune sought the other scale ;
Flags waver'd to and fro.
Oh ! who will lose, or who will win,
Amid that dreadful strife and din,
No mortal wight can know.
But hark ! a new fierce battle-cry.

Loud shouts of "Notre Dame!" rose high,
And round the eastern slope
Earl Gloucester led his infantry
With Montfort's right to cope.
With him the lord of Elmley came,
And his four sons of martial fame;
"A Beauchamp! Beauchamp!" was their word,
As on the foe they fiercely spurr'd;
And fighting, while they loudly shout,
Soon put the enemy to rout.

'Mid bushes of the thorn and whin
A dreadful slaughter did begin;
The bravest men of Warwickshire,
By halberds smitten down, expire.
Their horns in Ardenne's wood no more
Shall rouse at morn the bristly boar;
The wolf may rob the shepherd's fold,
Nor fear again those hunters bold;
Nor shall they in a swift career
Again pursue the Dunsmore deer;
And fearless of their well-train'd hawk
The hern in Arrow's ford shall stalk.
Then, Robin Hood, thy archers true,
Who had their stubborn bows that morn
Against the Prince's horsemen drawn,
In rapid flight withdrew,
To aim in greenwood at the harts
The remnant of their feather'd darts.

I

Prince Edward saw the foeman flee,
And to Sir Walter said in glee,
" Let us their wreck complete;
Ride swift, and bid Sir Roger lead
His horsemen through the western mead,
And cut off their retreat."
They met them, as, before the blast,
The thistle-down is driven fast:
Those who did flee were soon dispers'd,
Each sought to save his own life first;
Some to the Abbey precinct fled,
And with their blood the cloister steep'd;
Some into Avon's current leap'd,
And stain'd the river red.

So while they struggle did maintain
With the stream swollen by the rain,
The arrows reach'd them from the shore,
And many in the water died;
And Avon, floating corpses bore,
To tell to Tewkesbury how the pride
Of Montfort's army was no more.
Some safely gain'd the further side,
And fled, nor stay'd until afar
They left behind the sounds of war;
Northward, to Alcester, others post,
In hope to meet young Simon's host;
But they so hotly were pursued
And hack'd to death, their bodies strew'd

Lay like the leaves when autumn's gale
Strips the tall elms in Avon's vale.

But I must now war's tale suspend,
And sing of Walter's gentle friend.
Hoping in vain for tidings good,
Brought Isabel despairing mood.
News came Sir Walter and his men
Had pass'd one morn through Lymbroke's glen.
"Why came he not to Wigmore's gate,
Where she his coming did await?"
She said, and pined, and her cheek grew
Sunken, and thin, and pale of hue.
Desiring of her fate to know,
She often through the copse would go,
Until she came where fountain bright,
Near Brampton, show'd the pebbles white
Through its clear crystal, 'neath the shade
That branches of an old oak made;
And there would drop a little pin
The circle of the water in,
And ask the sprite who did reside
In the pure depth, "Shall I be bride
Of him for whom I long have sigh'd?"
If to the surface bubbles rose,
Her heart, a moment, felt repose;
But if no watery answer came
She did her cruel fortune blame.

At morn and eve she sought the aisle
Of Wigmore's fair monastic pile,
And there before the image pray'd
Of the blest Virgin, for her aid.
The morn succeeding to the fight,
Soon as the sun's returning light
Restored the blue and red to flowers,
And verdant hue to hazel bowers,
She rose, and knelt near Lady Maud
In that dim place, and Heaven implored
Her friend might be to her restored.
The Abbot, as to mass he went,
Seeing the maiden on her knee,
Telling her beads of rosary,
And gazing down so mournfully,
A look of pity on her bent;
And thought, "She for some soldier pleads,
Who haply now in battle bleeds;
Unless some joyful news come here
She soon will rest upon her bier."

Not long she knelt upon the stone,
Murmuring her prayer in mournful tone,
When suddenly she heard a heel
Press heavily the porch's floor;
And saw, pass through the Gothic door,
A warrior clad in links of steel.
"The news hath come at last," she thought.
"What are the tidings he hath brought?"
But lo! his lifted spear-point bears

A ghastly head with hoary hairs.
As up the nave the soldier trod,
The brow he rear'd aloft did nod ;
Within her breast quick throbb'd her heart,
And Lady Maud did soon upstart.
The warrior said : " Thy husband's gift,
De Montfort's head, my lance doth lift.
Look ! 'tis the haughty tyrant's frown,
He and his host we have o'erthrown."
And then into a sack of cloth
He plunged his hand, beside his belt,
And for some other trophy felt,
Then drew two palms, all bloody, forth.

He wav'd the hands, shorn from the wrist.
All did at that same moment list
The tinkling of a silver bell,
Which to the worshippers did tell,
Within the holy choir, the priest
Partook of the celestial feast.
Then Lady Maud sank on her knee,
In reverence of the Mystery,
And a great wonder seem'd to see.
The sever'd hands the warrior grasp'd
Appear'd in supplication clasp'd ;
She almost fainted at the sight,
And on her spirit dawn'd the light
That Montfort was a pious knight,
And his two folded hands show'd sense
Of what was due, and reverence

For holy things.   " O Thomas Clare ! "
(For he it was who held them there,
Earl Gloucester's valiant son and heir,)
" Take them," she said, " into the choir,—
The praying hands, and brow that frown'd,—
And tell the Abbot I desire
He bury them in holy ground."

Close to the screen, that carv'd of wood
Between the nave and chancel stood,
Clare bore the head and palms ;
And as when hawk soars o'er a grove
Are hush'd the warblers' songs of love,
So ceas'd the holy psalms ;
For when the monks beheld his spear
Over the screen the visage rear,
They started from their seats amazed,
And at the ghastly token gazed ;
But when they knew De·Montfort's look,
The piteous sight they could not brook ;
Over their eyes their cowls they thrust,
And wept the outrage to his dust.

De Clare the lady's message gave,
And bade the Abbot take the head
And hands, and place them in a grave,
And for the Earl a mass be said.
The Abbot from his stall of oak
Came forth, and to the warrior spoke :
" Bounds should be set to human hate ;

Cursèd are those who mutilate
The bodies of their enemies."
And then he rais'd to Heaven his eyes,
And said, "Let conquerors take heed;
When God His judgment Throne shall mount,
Both great and small shall give account
For every cruel deed.—
For head that hath so wisely plann'd
The freedom of our Church and land
The monks of Evesham will find room,
With Montfort's body, in one tomb;
They will revere the silent clod
From which the soul hath fled to God,
For never was a knight more true
To render Holy Church her due;
May God his one great sin forgive,
In that he dared from convent draw
And take the Lady Eleanor
In wedlock's bond with him to live."—
The trembling Abbot ended then,
And the monks groan'd a deep "Amen."

Clare then perform'd the dame's commands,
And laid the fragments in the hands
Of the good monk, who sorely griev'd,
And shudder'd as he them receiv'd;
But went, his soul grown still more large
With sense of greatness of his charge,
Toward the ledge with chalice graced,
And there the hero's relics placed;

And from the chancel came a strain
That echoed sadly through the fane.

"DIRGE.
"Saviour, listen to our dirge ;
By Thy sweating drops of blood,
By Thine anguish on the Rood,
From his sin the warrior purge.
Dona ei pacem.

"By Thy Blood that for us ran,
By Thy going through the gloom,
By Thy burial in the tomb,
His transgressions do not scan.
Dona ei pacem.

"By Thy Power the grave that shook,
By Thy Words to souls in pain,
By Thy coming back again,
Blot his sin from out Thy Book.
Dona ei pacem."

With solemn thoughts Clare left the fane
And found his weary steed again,
And led him forward by the rein,
And overtook the awe-struck dame
And friend, returning whence they came.
But while he walked the twain beside,
The matron ask'd how Montfort died,
And where the battle was decided,
And they were vanquish'd whom he guided.

"Man's eye," he said, "hath never seen
More dreadful fight than this hath been.
We met our foes near Evesham town,
And fought them on a furzy down;
We left upon the field eight score
Of rebel knights, drench'd in their gore.
The holy monks will have no dearth,
Of winter fuel for their hearth,
Their land is strewn with broken bows
And lances, splintered on our foes.
But you would hear of Montfort's fall.
Well! well! I now will tell you all.
From hour of prime to bell of tierce
The conflict raged both hot and fierce,
But when my father turn'd their right,
And with his force put them to flight,
De Montfort, seeing all was lost,
And victory favour'd Edward's host,
Blew a loud note upon his horn,
Which summon'd to his side a crew
Of knights, the bravest and most true,
Who rallied there of hope forlorn;
He made them in a circle form,
The better to abide the storm
Of horsemen, who were gathering round,
With sword and battle-axe, to wound,
And lay them dead upon the ground."

Montfort rode not his charger good,
(That had sunk down with loss of blood,)

But in the ring of warriors stood,
Who, all dismounted, placed their tread
Upon the bodies of the dead
That round about their ring were spread;
And the Earl's hands a sword did hold,
Prepared to give us welcome bold.
The air grew dark with wondrous gloom,
Through which his form more grand did loom—
More clearly seen when lightnings fly,
With thunders rattling in the sky,
As if had come the day of doom.

" Earl Gloucester cried unto our throng,
'Now charge against their chivalry;
The lightning lifts a torch to see
How to smite down our enemy—
The thunder leads our battle song;
At once rush forward to the slaughter,
Break through their close ring, give no quarter,
Put all the rebels to the sword.'
Loud as the thunder thus he roar'd,
And by his words to vengeance stirr'd
Our steeds against their spears we spurr'd.
At first our chargers fear'd to face
The weapon-guarded ring;
Red drops fell from their flanks apace
Beneath the rowels' sting,
They shied away from shouts and blows,
But still we urged them on the foes,

At whose mailed heads our axes dash'd,—
Our armour with their blood was splash'd.

" As one by one the warriors fell,
He boasted loud with savage yell ;
But o'er our shouts De Montfort's rose,
Bidding his knights their circle close.
' Guy Baliol, hold my banner fast,
Let it wave o'er us till the last.'
But, Lady, thy brave husband's sword
The standard bearer's bosom gored,
And with him sank the ensign proud;
I saw it wrap him as a shroud.
A part in the fierce strife I claim :
From Bohun's helm I hack'd the swan,
And from his vizor red blood ran.
But I will not attempt to name
All who there help'd the foes to tame ;
Suffice to say how weapons clave
The armour of Ralph Basset brave,—
Astley, Guy Montfort, Revelé,
De Vesci, Hopville, Crespigny
Fell down, and made the ring grow less,
And brought De Montfort more distress.

" Not Hugh Despenser e'en was saved,
England's chief justice' conduct pure
Could not his life from us secure,
So fiercely he behaved.
Mauleverer more like a fiend

Than any there himself demean'd.
Two youths, who had been captives ta'en,
Were by his cruel falchion slain,
Both of a tall and graceful form—
John Beauchamp and De Mandeville ;
They to his mercy made appeal,
But found him ruthless as the storm.
Compassion then my wrath allay'd
As I those youthful knights survey'd,
Lie, like two rosebuds by a shower
Beat down beside some ruin'd tower.

" From Leicester e'en remonstrance darts.
' Is there no pity in your hearts ? '
' For a seducer there is none,'
My father cried.   ' See, we have won ;
Arch-rebel ! now submit at last,
And at our feet thy falchion cast.'
' Dogs ! traitors ! I no mercy crave,'
He answer'd ; ' give me but a grave ; '
And with both hands his sword he rais'd,
At his great strength all were amaz'd ;
Two men could scarce that blade uplift,
He whirl'd it as a plaything swift,
Nor seem'd to feel its load.
Where'er that two-edged weapon dash'd
Sparks from the shattered armour flash'd
And blood in torrent flow'd.
Twelve gallant knights to death he smote ;
Red grew his armour and surcoat.

" But now the day turned dark as night,
Scarce could we see our foes to smite ;
The sun, it seem'd, would hide his face
In terror from that slaughter-place.
So loudly did the thunder roar,
There might have been in heaven a war ;
But suddenly—there came a crash,
The earth beneath me reel'd,
That instant fell a livid flash
That lit up all the field.
I saw it all, I saw it plain,—
The pools of blood, the heaps of slain
And wounded, writhing in their pain,
And broken spear and shield.
But when the flash the sky that burn'd
Had pass'd away, and gloom return'd,
I heard a cry, 'It is God's grace,'
And through the thick and murky air,
That made all look more dreadful there,
I saw the Earl lie on his face ;
Blood oozed his shoulder-blades between,
From wound made by a falchion keen ;
Who from behind him struck the blow,
And laid the mighty Baron low,
Haply no one will ever know ;—
He sense of chivalry did lack,
Who secretly did pierce his back."

Then Lady Maud said, " I rejoice
That hush'd is now the tyrant's voice ;

Prince Edward wins his own again,
And good King Henry now will reign."
When Isabel heard all the tale,
She shudder'd, and her face grew pale ;
For in her heart she felt a fear
Lest she more dread report might hear,—
The death or wound of one most dear.
But Wigmore's dame said, " Montfort's son,
Young Simon, ere the fight was done
Led he his troop from Kenilworth
To face our royal army's wrath ? "
To her the warrior, smiling, said,
" Oh ! he too long at Alcester stay'd,
And o'er his morning meal delay'd ;
When we had ceas'd our foes to kill
We saw him, from a neighbouring hill,
On horseback scan the battle ground,
And raise his hand toward the sky,
And dash it down against his thigh,
As if he felt deep agony ;
Then turn his charger quickly round,
And giving him a loosen'd rein
Swift gallop out of sight again.
May ne'er be mine that knight's remorse,
Who rode away upon that horse,
For had he hurried on his host
His sire might not the day have lost."

Conversing thus they cross'd the moat,
And through the portal's gloomy throat

Came into Wigmore's Castle-yard.
Clare gave his charger to a guard,
And Lady Maud went to provide
Refreshment after his long ride ;
But Isabel the soldier led
Into the empty hall, and said,
"Hath Lady Maud's late guest been spared,
Or hath he in the slaughter shared ?—
The youthful knight, who hither came ;"—
Her modesty and maiden shame
Forbade her speak her loved one's name.

De Clare replied, "The youth was slain."
"What dost thou say? Is *his* blood shed ?
Shall I not see his face again ? "—
And from her cheek the colour fled,
And she sate like one turn'd to stone.
At length inquir'd in mournful tone,
"Gave he no message e'er he died
To one who hoped to be his bride ? "
"Yes, dying, he breathed out farewell
To thee he called his Isabel."
" O my good Clare ! then he was mine !"
A wild light in her eyes did shine.
"Control thy grief, thy mind compose ;
There is a comfort in his fall ;
He made of life a noble close,
Doing great deeds before us all.
One of the first he fell, but rose
And battled bravely with his foes ;

But while he fought one dealt a blow
That bent him to the saddle-bow;
He vainly tried to keep the selle;
His fingers loosed the guiding rein,
And from his charger down he fell;
I heard him moaning in his pain,
'A long adieu, my Isabel.'

"We laid him on a soldier's bier,
Prince Edward shedding many a tear;
And of our host, the noblest four
His corpse to Evesham Abbey bore.
The prior met us at the gate,
And, pitying the young knight's fate,
Walk'd at the long procession's head
With his cross-bearer; following them
Paced monks, who sang a requiem.
Behind the body, two and two,
Came the brave leaders of our crew,
While waxen tapers lit the gloom.
I saw him laid within the tomb
Before St. Ecgwin's altar high,
The Prince and Monarch standing by,
And not a single visage dry.
The good monks vow no day shall pass
But they will chant for him a mass
Who lies in grave beneath their feet
Where they sing daily anthems sweet,
And that their painted window pane

His honour'd 'scutcheon shall contain ;
Therefore from fruitless grief refrain."

When Isabel the news receiv'd
She trembled, and her bosom heav'd
And sank ; then from her lips there burst
This cry, " I fear'd, I dream'd it oft ;
Before thou spak'st I knew the worst,—
That he would be in danger first,
And so would die Sir Walter Croft."
" What say'st thou ? " answer'd Thomas Clare ;
" I never told thee *he* was dead ;
Thou might'st have saved thee this despair ;
He lives, his chosen one to wed."
" O yes ! he lives in Heaven," she sigh'd,
" Where I shall hope to be his bride.
Show me the way, I will not halt,
But haste to die upon his vault."

"Such outrage to thy life forego,
There is no reason for thy woe.
His spirit hath not taken flight ;
He is our army's boast, that knight.
I spoke of our brave foe,
Earl Leicester's son, Sir Henry, who
To Wigmore's fortress came with you,
And for your love did vainly sue."
A heavy load fell from her heart,
And yet the tidings brought a smart ;
She could not hear and not feel ruth

At death of that bold generous youth.
Could he have, living, heard her sigh,
He would not have so longed to die.

But Isabel once more begun :
"Indeed, I sorrow for the knight
Whose fortune early death did blight ;
But thou didst say Sir Walter won
Great fame."　"He search'd for it as if
It fairest bloom'd on danger's cliff,
And won it.　He the Monarch brought
From midst of foes with whom he fought ;
The Prince declared his gratitude."
Then tears of joy her cheek bedew'd.
"I knew when came the last great fight
That he would on the rock of time
Engrave another deed sublime.
But tell me, Clare, for my delight,
How Edward prais'd that youthful knight?"
"He said, 'For sure, no soldier braver
Better deserv'd reward or favour.'

"After the Earl had met his doom
The dusky clouds to Cotswold steer'd,
Then the bright sun again appear'd
And scatter'd all the gloom ;
And, arch'd above the Lenches' ridge,
Was seen a rainbow's colour'd bridge.
The awful tempest now was past,
It to the battle's close did last,

Ever increasing in its strength ;
We joy'd it died away at length ;
Not but that distant thunder's moan
Answer'd the dying soldier's groan.
The earth, which blood and rain did soak,
Began beneath the warmth to smoke.
Now glittering in the light we spied
The royal banner waving wide.
Clad in blue tabards, laced with gold,
The trumpeters to lip did hold
Their clarions, hung with flags enscroll'd,
And sounded for the victory.
And then the King and Prince we see,
Riding together to the hill,
Whose slope for nigh the space of rood
Was strewn with bodies, and the blood
Ran down in ruddy rill.

" King Henry check'd his charger's rein
And gazed upon the warriors slain ;
But when Earl Leicester's corpse he spied
Among the dead, he deeply sigh'd.
' He who once filled my soul with dread,
Lo ! in the dust he lieth dead.
He aim'd to make his two-edged sword
A sceptre, and to rule his lord ;
But alter'd is his haughty style ;—
He who would govern England's isle
Now holds of it no more of space
Than six long feet of ground,

Nor hath he force yon fly to chase
That buzzes o'er his wound.
The prayer of saintly men prevails :
To the good brethren's suit at Hales
(Whose fane he ope'd few month's ago,
With lordly pomp, and regal show)
This glorious victory we owe ;
And the red drops of precious blood
The Saviour shed upon the Rood,
Which Richard to their Abbot gave,
Have made *one* soldier still more brave.
But oh ! to see my standard pitch'd
In soil with English blood enrich'd :
How stout of heart those Barons were
The steel to face, and death to dare,
And now—to see them lying there !'

" But Edward thus bespoke his sire :
'These moments other task require ;
They who have met our arms with force,
Deserve not from thy heart remorse.
But of the helpers of our cause,
Though some have pass'd beyond reward
Of knighthood, and of acres broad,
And hear not our applause,
Yet they who have survived the feud
Demand our warmest gratitude.
The sweetest office of this hour
Establishing our royal right,
Is to repay each earl and knight

Of signal valour in the fight ;
O grant to me this power !'
'Thou hast it, on this golden day, •
When we have made a history
To last through all eternity.'
Then Edward thus to me did say :
'Call him who led my sire away
From out the fury of the strife,
And guarded well his sacred life.
Go, seek him where yon troop is rank'd ;
Invite him hither to be thank'd.'
When I departed, many a lord
And many a knight from weary steed
Dismounted, and stood on the mead
Supported by his sword.

" Riding on charger white as snow,
Save where the crimson spots did show
That blood had spurted from a blow,
To meet the Prince Sir Walter came.
His hack'd shield and rent armour told
How he had faced the strong and bold,
His batter'd helmet said the same ;
His vizor rais'd, he look'd to be
The flower of England's chivalry.
Behind him paced a captive, bound,
His spear had stricken him to ground ;
I heard he was Llewellyn styled,
A chieftain's son, from Idris wild.

" The grateful Prince rode nigh, and shook
Sir Walter's mailèd hand,
And said, 'Thou hast a modest look,
But well canst wield thy brand.
Thou to our cause wert ever leal,
And true as thy well-proven steel.
I well remember thy white flag
Once beckon'd me to Dinmore crag.
Now, when my father falsely dight
In Montfort's armour might, mista'en,
Have in that traitor's stead been slain,
Thou acted'st like true knight.'
We waved the sword, we waved the spear,
And rais'd for both a mighty cheer."

" ' Yes,' said the King, 'God in the skies,
Who doth confound the strong and wise,
Far, far beyond my weak desert
By him deliver'd me from hurt.'
But Edward : 'For thy succour lent,
If thou canst win the maid's consent,
The fairest face, the wealthiest hand
Under our ward thou mayst command.'
' My Prince, the motive for my deed
Looked higher than a golden fee,
Or lovely maid with dowery ;
The act itself was my true meed.'
While the youth spake, a crimson glow
Flush'd o'er his face up to his brow,
And then one hand, as half afraid,

He lifted, where his helm display'd
A little tress of golden hair,
Which blows upon that helm did spare,
And said, 'Let this my love declare;
The brow from whence this lock I shore
Hath like a banner gleam'd before
My spirit in the shock of war.'

"The Prince replied, 'I much commend
Thy constancy to one dear friend,
I felt the same strong love before
I wedded with my Eleanor;
But tell me, how is styled the maid?'
'Her name is Margaret Meredith,
She's poor, but I have loved her sith
I met her in wild Whitecliffe's shade.'
The captive who behind him stood
Heard Walter's speech in mournful mood;
His fettered hand I saw him rear,
And from his pale cheek brush a tear;
I'm sure the maid to him was dear."

Clare stopp'd, for he perceiv'd his words
Hurt Isabel, like sharpen'd swords;
She press'd her hand against her heart,
To dull the pain that there did dart.
"When will be knit the marriage bond?"
She asked in tone of deepest sorrow.
De Clare replied, "They wed to-morrow.
Indeed he must be lover fond;

With palm scarce cleansed from bloody stain
He will her plighted hand obtain.
The Prince desired it should be so;
And said the rebel Hopville's land
Should dower the lovely maiden's hand,
That all his gratitude might know."
"But where will the young pair be wed?"
"In Dinan Castle's fane," he said;
"Prince Edward promised to attend
The marriage of his loyal friend."

"Thanks to thy courtesy, brave youth,
In thus unfolding all the truth;
Thy words have given me a wound
For which, methinks, no cure is found."
So spake she, and could scarcely draw
Her breath;—for anguish heard no more,
But, summoning her shatter'd strength,
Stagger'd adown the chamber's length,
And hurried through the door;
With both hands grasp'd her glossy hair,
As down it stream'd upon her shoulder;
And, wishing no eye to behold her,
Swift scaled the turret stair.

She gain'd her room, and gave relief
With flood of tears to her deep grief;
And, seated on a ledge of stone,
Within the window's deep-splay'd wall,
On which the rays of morning fall,

Thus murmur'd to herself alone :
" I knew not Margaret's love was offer'd
At the same shrine where mine I proffer'd—
The world for me is full of gloom ;
The roses of my life are borne,
Alas ! upon a canker'd thorn,
And will not come to bloom.
I would I had resigned life's powers,
And lay beneath the churchyard flowers."

While musing thus she heard a knock,
And fingers firm revolv'd the lock ;
And Lady Maud came in, and said,
" Indeed I pity thee, poor maid ;
I know what doth thy heart convulse—
From Walter thou hast met repulse ;
By scornful message Clare hath given,
I know thy tender heart is riven."
" Yes, he on whom my love was set
To-morrow weds my Margaret ;
Such tie indeed my heart doth grieve."
" Yet I did lately news receive,"
Said Lady Maud, " I dared not tell,
That he met her in Lymbroke's dell ;
The flowers in summer warmth will spring,
But his love ever was a thing
That would not ripen with the aid
Of radiant smiles thy cheek display'd."

But Isabel, who made a veil
With both hands for her visage pale,

Hung down her dark-tress'd head awhile,
And with a fit of sobbing shook,
And then raised up a mournful look,—
Smiled with a bitter smile.
Her glance fell on a vase which stood
Within the window's deep recess,
Where Provence roses, red as blood,
Display'd their loveliness.
She snatch'd a handful of the bloom,
Which filled with fragrance all the room,
And through the casement cast away
The petals on the winds to play.
She watch'd them whirling round and round,
Until they rested on the ground,
Then mournfully did say,
" Like ye, my youth's bright hopes are gone.
Oh! what for me is life now worth?
I have no comfort upon earth,
Now she his love hath won."

Quoth Lady Maud, " Thine eyelids dry ;
Be not one of the maids who die
Of hopeless love, so would not I.
God's sooth! when I was of thy years,
Had one who in me lit love's flame
Presumed to play *me* such a game
I had not shed weak tears ;
But I had acted braver part,
And with my poignard stabb'd his heart,
As Marion Bruyère slew her lover

In Dinan's tower of Pendover;
But thy soul is too weak I know
To serve a lukewarm lover so;
Then listen to a friend's advice,
Nor be deterr'd by scruples nice;
An act like his, is better borne
By boldly meeting scorn with scorn;
Sir Walter will not be thy mate,
Then change thy love for him to hate.

"Soon as to-morrow morn discloses
The colour of the blushing roses
I on my palfrey take my seat,
And ride to Dinan, there to meet
My spouse, who thither comes to-night.
If Clare hath told his message right
Resolve to travel in my train,
And visit thy old home again;
And, when thou art arrivèd there,
Command thy damsels to have care
To weave among thy raven curls
A precious string of ocean pearls;
Put a gold chain around thy neck,
Rich bracelets on thy smooth white arms,
And, by their art, thy virgin charms
With all that's beauteous deck;
And when the marriage rite hath ceas'd,
And hush'd is voice of holy priest,
And guests sit down at wedding feast,
Sit down with them, exert thine art

To wake love in some other heart;
Soon will thy beauty which God gave
Make some handsome youth thy slave.
Yes, banish sorrow from thy brows,
And all thy energy arouse,
And Thomas Clare may be thy spouse.
Let Walter see thee bravely bear
The loss of love he would not share."

With indignation then did swell
The loving heart of Isabel.
" May's bloom and summer's golden hours
Have pass'd with sunshine, song, and flowers,
Since first I set on him my gaze,
And hoped to spend with him my days.
That hope, O! how I foster'd it,—
It will not in a moment flit."
The matron gave a scornful look,
And down the stair her way she took
With hurried steps, and masculine.
But to herself the maiden said,
" She cannot fathom love like mine;
I never will another wed.
My love's a flower that only blows
But once,—and no more blossom shows."

The morn, whose genial radiance beat
Upon the chamber's window seat,
Where Isabel her fate deplor'd,
And converse held with Lady Maud,

Dawn'd too on Evesham's green hill-side,
Where lay of Montfort's host the pride.
From the stain'd slope, gorged with his food,
The wolf shrunk back into the wood;
The raven flew from forest oaks,
And o'er the scene of slaughter croaks;
The lark began from earth to soar,
And sing above the hill her song,
Which many a knight shall hear no more,
Stretch'd dead its gorse among.
In vain the sun shed down its glare
On eyes that look'd with stony stare,
It gave no warmth to cold limbs there;
But Christain love sent some to aid
The sufferers, lying on the ground;
The monks did from their Abbey stray
To bathe the brow, and salve the wound,
And with their cordials death delay.

They, kneeling down, receiv'd the shrift
Of sinners, and the Cross did lift
Before their fading eyes;
And when death came, a welcome friend,
Their last sad bitter pang to end
And make of them his prize,
They stripp'd the armour from the dead,
And reverently the cold limbs spread,
(Crossing the white hands on the breast,)
And laid the bodies in a wain,
Which then was drawn by bullocks twain

To graveyard near the Abbey fane,
A place of holy rest.
The great bell of the Abbey toll'd
For burial of the brave and bold.

But where the dead and wounded lay,
Two nuns with snowy veils were seen
Behind the monks to take their way;
The lofty form and noble mien
Of one of them, and her white dress,
Bespeak her Lymbroke's Prioress,
Who scorn'd to dwell in idleness
When soldiers were in such distress.
Under her wimple, white as snow,
Look'd forth the sorrow of her brow;
She, at her girdle, bore a Christ,
Of ivory workmanship unpriced;
With wounds in Hands, and Feet, and Side,
And Arms outspread,—the Crucified.
She carried in her hand an urn
Full of well-water, fresh and clear,
To wet lips that with fever burn:
The dying smiled as she drew near.

She gave the cool pure draught to each
Whose glistening eyes her help beseech,
But started, when amid her toil
She saw red blood her sandals soil.
The raven rose up from his feast
Upon some slaughter'd man or beast,

And flew away, on pinion slow;
But still amid those scenes of woe
The nuns their holy work pursued.
They wash'd away the clotted blood,
And drew the arrow from the wound,
Then lifted up the blessed Rood,
And many, gazing, comfort found.
"Look up to Jesus, on Him rest,
He will receive thee to His breast."—
What horrid forms of death were there!
What moans of pain, shrieks of despair!
A son lay dying near his sire,
And curs'd him for his former ire;
A brother, struck by brother's blow,
Who was himself by him laid low,
Look'd on the body by his side,
And triumph'd with unnatural pride.
The horses shared their masters' pain,—
Could scarce their agony sustain,
And furious roll'd upon the mead
To free their flank from feather'd reed.

But soon the kind recluses saw
A sight for pity and for awe,
Where dark-robed kneeling monks did draw
The armour from a headless trunk,
And all the while were weeping sore
For him whose blood the earth had drunk;
But suddenly their hands they rais'd,
And shouted, "Arm of God be prais'd!

Look at the hair shirt, red with gore,
Between his habergeon and skin,—
The pious Earl this sackcloth wore
In penance for his sin.
May the red bolt the butcher scorch,
Who slew the Champion of our Church !"

The nuns said, " May he be forgiven
For marrying a bride of Heaven."
And soon they came where, 'mid the gorse,
A Chief lay near his slaughter'd horse,
And drew half-stifled breath.
The pious sisters felt a joy
That they may now their skill employ
In saving him from death.
Loosen'd his vizor to give air,
The west wind on his pale cheek blew,
And then a stronger breath he drew
One from his forehead mov'd the hair,
That he might better feel the gale.
A change came o'er his visage pale,
He ope'd his eyes, and wildly stared ;
His fever'd lip did not refuse
The water from their earthen cruse.
His bleeding side they then unbared,
Where, next the ribs, a sword had press'd,—
The wound with lint and salve they dress'd.

His bosom broad did heave and pant,
And a strange look reveal'd a want

To tell some secret to the nun,—
Some lawless act which he had done.
Thrice he sate up and strove to speak,
Thrice backward sank his body weak.
Compassioning his misery,
The Prioress laid on her knee
His head, and downwards bow'd to hear
What hidden guilt he would disclose
Before that death, approaching near,
Should end his bitter woes.
"Lady," he said, "I have in time
Committed many a glaring crime,
Of which, as my death draweth nigh,
My soul is wrung in memory.
My sins oppress me with a power,
Unknown before this dying hour;
For many I cannot atone,
But I can make amends for one."

He stopp'd, his breath began to fail;
She fann'd his forehead with her veil,
And then, in accents weak and low,
He said: "A score of years ago
A Cambrian band under my order
Made foray on the English border;
From many a castle which we fired
The smoke and flame to heaven aspired.
Beside his hearth a knight I slew,
But looking on his lovely child,
Who at my dripping falchion smiled,

A touch of pity knew;
I gave her to one of my band
To bear her safe to my own land.
In Bradwen hall the infant play'd,
And sported by Arthog's cascade,
And grew to be a lovely maid.
My minstrel taught her Gwynedd songs,
And all that to his art belongs.
But when Llewellyn, my brave son,
Was by her full-blown beauty won,
And she his suit denied,
I led her to De Genville's fort
To be with his own daughter taught,
And there she doth abide.
I heard her mother took the veil,
And dwells in Lymbroke's peaceful dale.
Oh! by thy Christian charity,
Let some one to the good nun tell
Where now her beauteous child doth dwell;
Grant this last boon to me."

The Prioress trembled with surprise,
For she remembered well the night
When flamed her castle to the skies,
And her babe vanish'd from her sight.
She bent her ear down to his lip,
Who now was in death's awful grip.
"O! art thou he my spouse who slew,
And took away my infant too?
God's vengeance finds the murderer out;

But still, the joyful news I doubt."
The dying warrior feebly smiled.
" Then thou art she I sought to find
To give to her embrace her child,
And die with calmer mind."
" Yes, I am Lymbroke's nun," she said,
" But yet I doubt the happy news."
" If credence thou wilt still refuse,
Unloose at once the silken thread,
That binds a little cross of gold
Upon my bosom, 'twill be proof
The story that I now have told
Is not of falsehood's woof."
She waited for no second word,
But snapp'd in twain the silken cord,
And seized the cross hung from his neck ;
It was the same her babe did deck
When on her brow gleam'd chrisom-drops,
And she felt all a mother's hopes.
" Tell me," she cried, " the castle's name
Which thou didst fiercely set aflame."
The dying Chief, in whisper soft,
Replied, " It bore the name of Croft."
" My long lost daughter then is found,"
She said, and sank upon the ground.
Her friend with water bathed her brows,
And tried her dormant sense to rouse.
The warrior cast a look to Heaven,
And to his spirit peace was given.

The cool drops roused the Prioress soon
To life and motion from the swoon,
But when she saw the dead man lie,—
"O! where," she cried, "O! where am I?"
"Whose is this body on the soil?"
But as her memory came again
Of all he told her in his pain,
"We must," she said, "now leave our toil;
There is a fever in my breast;
I cannot work, I cannot rest,
Until my new-found daughter lies
Where once were stilled her infant cries.
O! for some wings my form to lift
And carry me to Dinan, swift."
She on the blood-stain'd earth sate down;
While peasant, who for plunder sought
The battle-field, their palfreys brought
From hostel in the town.
She gave to him a piece of gold
Who led her steed, and rein did hold.
O! what was gold to her that hour,
When cherish'd hope bore precious flower.

Far from the sound of steed's wild neigh
That on the field in torture lay,
Far from the sound of warrior's groan,
They travell'd to the forest lone
Of Feckenham.   All seemed so still:
Here oaks umbrageous crown'd a hill;
And here, the ancient stems between,

Expanded spacious glades of green,
Where wild kine grazed, or timid crowd
Of deer rose silent as a cloud,
And vanish'd in among the trees ;
There was no sound but of the bees.
In a green plot, clear'd of the wood,
The cottages of Rous Lench stood.
A hound from one, on crippled claw,
Maim'd that he might not chase the deer,
Limp'd forth ; the Prioress dropt a tear,
And blamed the cruel forest law
Which sanction'd such a pitiless deed ;
And soon again her heart did bleed,
When one asked alms who was made blind
For slaughter of a dappled hind.

Their road by Kington village lay ;
It was an open greensward way,
And led by palisaded hay,
Whither the hunters drove with hound
And horn the beasts that roam around,
And them with their keen arrows shot.
But on they rode, and reach'd a spot
From whence the ancient oaks recede,—
A sunny and fern-cover'd mead,
To which in spring the bustards came,
And to the place had given their name.
And here they found a cause for fear,
For in the open space appear
Full forty men in Kendal green,

And in their hands yew-bows were seen;
The feathers in the caps were torn,
Their jerkins' hue with blood was steep'd,
From quivers at the baldrick borne
A few plumed arrows peep'd.
The leader stepp'd before his band,
And with a tone of firm command
Inquir'd " why the recluses stray'd
Without an escort through the glade."
The Prioress told what work for God
They did on Evesham's bloody sod;
And why they left the field in haste,
And travell'd through the woodland waste.

" If you our wounded did attend,
Ladies, in me you find a friend.
The day will soon draw to a close;
'Tis perilous for such as you
To wander here, like timid does;
Your guide shall be one of our crew,
Who every forest track doth know.
Ho ! Trossel, with these ladies go,
And them by shortest pathway guide
To Westwood, where some nuns reside,
Who hold the rule of Fontevraux,
And to help strangers are not slow;
Their hospitable convent stands
On th' edge of these wild forest lands.
Unguided, you may miss your way,
And in the night to wolves be prey;

And there are robbers in the wood
Who will not act so kind as he."
He pointed where a gibbet stood
On spot from thicket free,
And there a thief was hung in chains
Rotting to pieces with the rains.
" Many like him, of harden'd soul,
Among these desert woodlands stroll."

" But sure, some hermit offers prayer
For them who through the forest fare ;
The Virgin will of us take care.
But who art thou, so kind and good?"
"I am the outlaw, Robin Hood,
The rich man's scourge, the poor man's shield,—
I to the weak a succour yield.
We in the cause of Montfort strove,
And many found a bloody bed
Before with our strong bows we fled
To strike the deer in grove.
Farewell, and may'st thou find thy child."
So they were led by pathway wild,
Until, when fell the shadows dark,
And on the moss shone glow-worm's spark,
And evening air grew damp and cool,
They to the place of refuge came,
And were receiv'd by noble dame
Who o'er the house bore rule.
There through the night the nuns did stay,
Till dawn'd fair Margaret's marriage day.

CANTO VI.

THE MARRIAGE.

THE bridal morn, that like a star
Shines for the maiden from afar,
But, when to her it draweth near,
Doth ever mingle hope with fear,—
That morning now for Margaret gleams,
All radiant with sunny beams.
It finds her in her turret-bower,
Awaiting the auspicious hour.
What are thy thoughts, dear gentle dove?
Dream'st thou of days of early love?
Or, flush'd with hope, dost thou surmise
Beyond the golden gate
Of marriage opes a paradise—
A still more blissful fate?
Now while thy life's first stages end
Do solemn musings thee attend,
Like petals of a summer rose,
That breathe a fragrance ere they close.
Why, as thou puttest on thy dress
For marriage, seem'st thou in distress?
'Tis not because love's spring is o'er,
That from thine eyes the teardrops pour.

Thou had'st a fearful dream last night,—
A form appear'd, array'd in white,
And with stern tone denounced the rite
That thee with Walter will unite.
Therefore, though sounds the bridal song
In the courtyard below,
Grave thoughts into thy bosom throng,—
A cloud is on thy brow ;
A strange mysterious dread alloys
The promise of thy coming joys.

But now once more the scene I change ;—
My song to Isabel shall range.
When she at night her belt unbraced,
And bodice of her robe unlaced,
And lay down on her couch, she wept,
And often ask'd, " What shall I do ?
Shall I my Margaret's wedding view ? "
But by and bye she slept,
And to her also came a dream.
She in a fane appear'd to be,
Among a goodly company
That met for marriage-rite did seem ;
When suddenly a glorious cloud
Descended on the festive crowd ;
And then, from out its sunny fold,
Array'd in robe glistering like gold,
An angel bent, and took the ring
The bridegroom for the bride did hold,
And to the sleeper it did bring.

She woke, and her bright pleasure fled,
But left good purpose in its stead;
She will do all that duty taught;
So rose, and rode to Dinan's fort.
But, as in Lawrence' belfry chime
The marriage bells at morning prime,
Her heart was sad with thought.
" O ! not for me is the delight
Of wedding-hour so exquisite;
Justly, no doubt, I have been slighted,
And my affection unrequited.
It argued me a maid unchaste
To seek his love with so much haste;
I should have worn a closer mask,
And not appear'd his hand to ask.
But why blame I my friend's neglect?
My scorn De Montfort's young life wreck'd.

But look the fane of fashion round,
That still in Dinan's ward is found
In chapel shorten'd of its apse
By storms, and war, and ages' lapse,—
For Margaret's marriage scene is crown'd
With flowers that shed a rich perfume,
The incense of their summer bloom.
The maidens who wait in her bower
Have deck'd the church with many a flower,
The ornament of wood and field,
And every sweet the gardens yield.
Carnations of the richest dyes;

Forget-me-nots, like Margaret's eyes ;
White lilies, that in shady places
Uplifted their meek modest faces ;
Chrysanthemums, with flowers of gold,
That August's fiery beams unfold.
And Isabel has stripp'd a bush
Of roses, like her own sweet blush ;
And, though her heart was still distress'd,
She had with them the altar dress'd.
Flowers round the window-arches clung,
And in festoons from rood-loft hung.

The circle of the church was fill'd
With those whom expectation thrill'd
To see the knot of marriage tied
Between Sir Walter and his bride ;
And many came there to evince
Their homage to the conquering Prince,
Who in the chapel took his place,
The wedding of his friend to grace.
Throng in the Barons, Earls, and Lords,
And knights and squires,—there scarce is room ;
In peaceful garb, but girt with swords,
Their different stations they assume.
All of them had been at the wars ;
Some faces there were seam'd with scars,
Prick'd with the spear through visor-bars ;
Some, wounded, leant upon their staves,
And thought of their dead comrades' graves.
De Althiley, and brave L'Estrange,

Who oft repell'd the Welsh, who range
To harry Verniew's fertile strand ;
The Earl of Hereford, Bohun,
(Sad for the treason of his son,)
Fitz Alan from the banks of Clun,
Knight Hospitaller of St. John,
From Ludford, nigh at hand ;
De Mortimer and Gilbert Clare,
The lords of wooded Knighton fair,
Of Brampton, Knucklass, and of Knill,
And Stapleton's strong castled hill,
Of Stokesay, Lingen, and Presteign,
Among those loyal chiefs were seen.

Above the arches interlaced,
Around the circle of the fane
A well-carved oaken gallery placed
Did lovely forms contain ;
Its seats were full as they could be
With ladies of a high degree.
The lustre of their jewels play'd
On neck, and arm, and tresses'-braid,
As leaning o'er the balustrade
They graciously bestow'd their glances
On knights, who throng'd the floor,
And lately steep'd their swords and lances
In foeman's crimson gore.

Now to the sanctuary turn your gaze,
Where, on the altar, vessels blaze

Of silver, richly wrought, and gold ;
And Wigmore's Abbot you behold.
An alb and cope, glittering all o'er
With golden thread, the Churchman wore ;
The lines of care upon his cheek
His grief for Montfort's death bespeak.
The bridegroom waits near to the porch ;
His mantle of a scarlet grain,
Wore o'er a vest of azure stain,
Appears the air to scorch ;
His robe is girdled with a sash
Whereon the richest jewels flash,
The grateful Monarch's gift ;
The thoughts that make his spirit glow
Are character'd upon his brow,
All clearly read their drift,—
A faith that he has come to meet
One who will make his life complete.
And yet sometimes doth pass a shade
Across his features, when awake
The recollection of Crusade
He solemnly had vowed to make,
And of the hermit's menace grave
He utter'd, standing by his cave,
On all who earthly things allow
To stay fulfilment of their vow.

Sweet flutes now fill'd with silvery sound
The compass of that temple round ;
The music told the hour was come.

From lip to lip there went a hum,
And then the veilèd bride was seen
Upon De Genville's arm to lean.
Some smiling girls, from baskets, shed
Handfuls of flowers before her tread.
She enters like a timid fawn
That fears to cross the open lawn;
Her blushes burn through the thin gauze,
That o'er her modest face she draws;
She wears a seymar white as snow,
Whereon the threads of silver glow;
The colour of her mantle vies
With the pure azure of the skies.
Pale jasmine and white roses spread
A graceful wreath around her head.
Poor Isabel, to show her love,
The flowers into a garland wove,
And, as she twined them, often wet
With her own tears the coronet.
Thoughts of her vision scares the bride,
As she stands by Sir Walter's side;
She fears to see the garment gleam
Of her who threaten'd in her dream.

Behind her gentle maidens stand,
Each with a posy in her hand;
But one among that beauteous group
Doth, like a storm-beat lily, stoop;
Upon her brow a wreath reposes,
Woven of fragrant Provence roses.

'Tis Isabel, who scarce compress'd
The sad regrets within her breast.
The flowers quivering in her hand
Show'd feelings she could not withstand ;
Her downcast look appears to say,
" Yes, every hope hath pass'd away ;
Alas ! not mine to taste on earth
Joys that might cluster round his hearth."
And then she threw a look of plaint
Toward the picture of the Saint,
Bless'd Mary, hanging on the wall
Behind the altar, letting fall
Glance of affection, soft and mild,
Upon her rose-cheek'd beauteous child.
And a rash thought her soul defiled,
" Is this the boon which I did seek,
Kneeling before thy image meek ? "

But when her glance the bridegroom's met,
More bitter then was her regret.
O ! love like her's must ever last,
It cannot from the heart be cast.
A few more moments, and her ear
The bride's soft answer then will hear ;
A few more, and the ring will sever,
Except on casual greeting given,
Her hand from Walter's hand for ever ;
And, though it be the will of Heaven,
She cannot think of Margaret's bliss
And not her own lost pleasure miss.

In vain she tried to soothe her mind,
And view the scene with air resign'd.

The Abbot, with an acolyte,
Who from a censer swung a cloud
Of incense, now paced through the crowd,
And near the porch began the rite.
His hand a silver crosier rear'd,
Whose crook emboss'd with gems appear'd :
Then from his lip this summons fell,
Clear as the sound of silver bell :
" Know any in this fane wherefore
These faithful lovers may not give
A pledge in wedlock pure to live,
And share together worldly store
Till life's events with them be o'er ?"
And then he turn'd toward the pair
(The gallant knight, and lady fair,
Who stood beside each other there) :
" I charge ye both, if either know
A reason why this bond of love
Should not be seal'd on earth below,
And be endors'd in Heaven above,
That cause at once to show."
Trembled the folds of Margaret's veil,
And under it her face turn'd pale ;
Would it prove true, her fearful vision ?—
Now is the moment of decision.

The heart of Isabel beat fast ;
But scarce two rapid moments pass'd,

When, from the court-yard, rose a shout
Of crowd, that throng'd the fane about :
" Make room for her, who comes to stay
The holy rite—make way ! make way!"
Clearly was heard a thrilling cry,
And then these words, distinct and nigh,—
" By all the blessed saints forbear
The bridgeroom and the bride to mate
In wedlock earth and Heaven hate !
My son, wed not with her !"

As when some sentenced patriot hears
Around the scaffold jocund cheers,
Telling he is repriev'd,
So those forbidding accents fell
Upon the ear of Isabel,
And her sad mind reliev'd ;
For they a cause of hope declare,
That now contends with her despair.
The crowd dividing, left a space
For one with veil and snow-white cape,
And garments grey, a lofty shape,—
Who enter'd with a troubled pace.
Then Margaret thought, " O ! do I see
The semblance of that stately one
Who in my dream in white robe shone,
And frowning look'd on me ?"

But straight to her the lady flew—
The matron full of majesty—

Who had sent forth that piercing cry,
And from her face the thin veil drew,
And bent awhile her anxious glance,
Perusing Margaret's countenance;
The sense of others' presence gone,
She saw but her alone.
The Abbot's face was calm, yet stern;
De Genville knit his shaggy brows,
Prince Edward's cheeks with wrath did burn,
The bridegroom more impatient grows.
The lady then threw back her hood,
And lo! near him his mother stood!
Stood silently—and then she smiled,
And then exclaimed, " My child! my child!
Thank God that I have come in time
To save ye both from shameful crime.
O Margaret! I am thy mother;
Thou wert about to wed thy brother."
" I thought my mother long since died,
But often, often wish'd she might
Return from Heaven to lead me right."—
" And I have come to be thy guide."

The maiden gazed upon her brow;
" Art thou alive, or from the dead?"
" Thou soon shalt feel my bosom glow;
No tears of joy do spirits shed."
And she fell on her daughter's neck,
And threw her arms around her waist,
Nor could her tears of pleasure check,

Adown her cheek they raced ;
And Margaret felt those tear-drops warm,
And knew she clasp'd a living form.
The mother loosen'd her embrace,
And scann'd once more the wavering face,
Clasp'd her again, and kiss'd her cheek,
And, growing calmer, thus did speak :
" Like to thy brother and thy sire
I see thee, and am doubly forced
To own thee as the child I lost ;
No further token I require ;
And yet to others may appear
Some sign desired to make it clear."

" Lay every proof before our eyes,"
Spake Edward ; " it may be surmise,
Born of a spirit overwrought
By vigil long and pious thought."
The happy mother then reveal'd
How, upon Evesham's battle-field,
She learnt from warrior, pierced by wound,
Where her lost daughter might be found ;
And drew out of her tunic's fold
That little jewell'd cross of gold
The warrior on his breast did bear.
" A certain proof I do not err,
For this I saw my infant wear ;
Now let the bride display her neck,
And if there be a little fleck,
Shaped like a rose, above her breast,

By that too she's my child confess'd."
Then Margaret's lovely face grew red
As she did what the matron said,
And now before them all unbared
Her beauteous neck, as ivory white,—
And lo ! a rose-shaped mole declared
The dame had spoken right.
" A dream that did my soul appal,"
Said Margaret, " which I now recall,
Was for my warning sent ;
I felt a yearning in my heart
That filial instinct doth impart,—
I now know what was meant."

Prince Edward said, "These signs have seal'd
The former evidence,—I yield."
The Abbot all the story heard,
And was with holy fervour stirr'd.
" Behold the mighty Hand of God !
His just reward, His righteous rod.
The robber-chief went on his path
Unconscious of the clouds of wrath
Gathering around God's mercy-seat,
But, all his sum of sins complete,
His death on Evesham-field did meet.
But the good nun, with kind intent,
Who from her cell at Lymbroke went
To roam the ruddy ground, and heal
The wounds carv'd by your cruel steel,
Heard tidings on that field of slaughter

That told her of her long lost daughter !
And look once more, this holy place
Was menaced with a foul disgrace,—
A marriage of incestuous kind ;
And lo ! this matron comes to free
The bridegroom and the bride and me
From cloud of guilt and infamy.
Reflect, O noble company !
Nor to God's ways be blind.
An angel-world surrounds us all,
And Heavenly voices speak in dreams ;
A mystery is what life we call,
Nor is the world just what it seems."
The Abbot trembled like a reed
Shaken by wind in Wigmore's mead ;
Partly it was the fault of age,
And partly hate of falchion's rage,
And cruelty in wars men wage :
At length he braced his English heart
Counsels of wisdom to impart,
And show the future scenes that rise
In glorious vision to his eyes.

" Now I have met thee face to face,
I will, my Prince, speak somewhat plain.
Upon thy 'scutcheon rests a stain,
And, knights, upon your shields disgrace ;
For, without mercy, blood was shed,
And outrage done unto the dead,
When you at Evesham triumphèd.

I call on you to expiate
This lust of cruelty and hate.
Look at your shields and surcoats cross'd
With the most holy sign ;
Let no more precious time be lost,
Obey these words of mine.
Wound not with strife your native land,
Whereon our fanes and Abbeys stand,
But sail for Palestine ;
And, from the Paynim, wrest the tomb
Where Mary's Son lay in the gloom
Till the third day did shine."

Then less severe his visage show'd,
Though still his speech with fervour glow'd :
" My Prince, thy rival is o'erthrown,
But make De Montfort's cause thine own ;
Nor follow a relentless hate,
But, like him, labour for the state.
With violence and shedding blood
Be not thy people's will withstood ;
First let them to thy council send
Their wisest,—and to them attend ;—
The English oak cannot be bent,
Although by storms it may be rent.

" The God within my soul awakes,
My mind a range more distant takes.
I bid thee not to sheathe thy sword,
But combat with thy foes abroad.

Oh ! if my vision tells me true,
Scotland and Wales thou shalt subdue,
And centre, in one mighty blaze,
Our Island-kingdom's fourfold rays ;
And, when thou hast succumb'd to fate,
On the united land shall wait
More glory, she shall grow more great.
I see the glimmer of her lance
Conquering amid the fields of France ;
And, looking down Time's long arcade,
I view, where'er her keels invade,
The tribes of earth more happy made.
Far in the ocean of the west
Lie regions now to us unknown,
There shall her sons set up their rest
When many years are flown ;
The races of the Indian land
Shall, peaceful, own her just command ;
And millions, after years of strife,
Shall owe to her a fuller life.
Go on, my Prince, be brave and wise,
List to the mandate of the skies ;
The stateliest bark requires the force
Of Heavenly gales to speed her course."

Prince Edward spake: "Well hast thou said ;
Thy solemn words shall be obey'd.
When we the embers of this war
Have quench'd, and civil strife is o'er,
We then will sail on our Crusade ;

And, if we are with victory bless'd,
My conquering leopards shall not rest,
But make for glory further quest.
The tribes of Cambria, who gave aid
To Montfort, well may be dismay'd,
For, by the grace of God most High,
I will fulfil thy augury."—
The Abbot now withdrew into the choir,
And all did from the holy fane retire.

The hour had come when mortals feel
Peace o'er their troubled nature steal,
And Margaret did her mother meet,
And brother ; and they found a seat
In Dinan's pleasance, in a bower.
The evening air was balmy sweet,
With scent of many a closing flower,
And all around were murmurings
Of home-bound bees, and whirr of wings
Of birds preparing for their rest
In bush or hedge, that held their nest.
The shouts of them whom revels please
In Dinan's court, came on the breeze
Softly and faintly to the ear ;
And in the meadow lowed the steer ;
Swallows with circling flight did sweep
On rapid pinion round the keep.
No flowery garland now was set
Upon the brow of Margaret,
Nor round her neck a golden chain ;

She said, as she had laid aside
These decorations of a bride,
And changed her marriage-robe for gown
Simple, and of a russet brown,
" I ne'er shall want these gauds again."

The Prioress took her children's hands,
(Bound now by tender kinship's bands,)
And said, " Indeed, I'm truly blest,"
And then her daughter she caress'd ;
" And art thou glad thou hast exchanged
A bridegroom for a loving brother?
Thou wilt not be from him estranged
If he should choose to wed another ;
All things are well arranged.
To me thou hast been born again
In joy, without a mother's pain ;
I always deem'd thou wast on earth,
And I should see thy second birth.
But, children, think what was my fear,
When one clad in a soldier's gear,
His armour all besmear'd with gore,
(He had from Evesham's victory fled,)
Came unto Westwood's convent-door,
And told ye would together wed !
How slowly dragg'd the hours of night ;
I never closed my weary eyes,
But watch'd till the first streaks of light
Told that the sun would soon arise ;
And ere his ray the earth relumed

My journey hitherward resumed.
At Redstone rock the stream ran broad,
My willing palfrey swam the ford;
Oh ! when from Whitcliffe's gentle height
I saw this fort, I bless'd the sight."

While thus she spoke, adown a walk
With rose-trees lined on either side,
Scenting the blossom on each stalk,
Fair Isabel did glide;
She had come there to calm her breast,
Which strange conflicting thoughts molest.
The same rose-wreath her forehead bears,
The same rich robe, and broider'd belt,
As when she at the marriage knelt,
Her graceful form still wears.
" Part of my dream has now come true;
Margaret, the ring is not for thee;
But I dreamt that the angel flew
And bore that gift to me,
And this may also be fulfilled."
So, fancy once more sought to build
A home which happiness should gild.

But Margaret noticed, and knew why
So wildly glanced her hazel eye,—
That love look'd from her eye and face,
That love was in that restless pace,
That fear did with her hope contend,—
So she felt pity for her friend;

And, in a heart affection warm'd,
Kind project suddenly she form'd.
" Look, yonder walks our Isabel,
Her thoughts, dear Walter, I know well ;
Our purposed marriage caused her grief,
But, interrupted, brings relief.
See, how she starts as there she strays,
Now lowers, now lifts to Heaven her gaze,
She thinks not that we watch her ways.
No doubt she would give worlds to know,
Now our betrothal is at end,
Whether thou wilt thy love bestow
On her, who is thy sister's friend.
I hope my speech may not offend,
But I have felt a jealousy
At what my neighbours said of thee,
That, since Prince Edward dubbed thee knight,
And she assisted at the rite,
Thou didst regard her more than me ;
And when thou heard'st one speak her name
Thy cheeks with blushes were aflame ;—
Such love-signs, *now*, I do not blame.

" Think not thy Margaret asks too soon
Of her new brother one small boon ;
Place in my hand the ring that thou,
In ignorance, brought me but now
To bind me to one bound before
By knot more strong than priest can draw.
If thou the ring to me wilt give,

And promise with my friend to live
In wedlock, I will soon revive
The colour in her visage pale,
And make o'er fear her hope prevail."
Sir Walter blush'd with love's own hue,
Nor heard his sister vainly sue,
Whose friend he loved, but had been loth
To break with Margaret his troth.
So he put forth to her his arm,
And laid the ring upon her palm.

She swiftly ran up to the maid,
Who down the pebbled pathway stray'd :
" O Isabel, for my dear sake
This present from my brother take."
And she held out her soft white hand,
And lo ! on it the golden ring ;
Then Isabel could scarce command
The joys that in her bosom spring !
" I heard love's wound to thee was dealt,
Who girded'st on my brother's belt,
And often read, as in a book,
Regard for him, in many a look."
Then Margaret threw her arm around,
Or Isabel had fall'n to ground ;
She trembled so, nor could believe
For joy the news her ears receive.
But Margaret on her finger placed
The ring, that might her own have graced ;
On the gold round she fixed her gaze,

"Then I must go to him," she says.
Now on the giver's arm she leant,
And toward the shady arbour went;
But Walter rose up from his seat,
And came the blushing pair to meet.

', Sister, in earlier day," he said,
"Before I set on thee my eyes,
Had I look'd on this beauteous maid
I might have made a choice more wise,
And sought from parent-stem to sever
This plant, to bloom near me for ever.
O Margaret! we both were blind
To ties that us together bind.
But, Isabel, wilt thou consent,
In place of thy dear friend, to come
And make an Eden in my home?"
A willing ear to him she lent;
A look of fervent love outstrips
The motion of her ruby lips,
Which, in a soft tone, whisper "Yes,"
And link him to her loveliness.

So after tossings on the sea
Of hopeless love's perplexity,
Joy came, in pure betrothal's bliss;
He seal'd her answer with a kiss,
And she return'd one warm and sweet;
And, as their loving lips did meet,
A loud, melodious song did gush

From tuneful throat of speckled thrush,
Perch'd on an ash-tree's graceful head,
Where hung the berried clusters red ;
It was a " good night " to the sun,
That slowly sank, his journey done,
Behind a cloud of orange hue,
And gold tints o'er the ramparts threw.
O Isabel ! now truthful seems
The happiest of all thy dreams !
When, in thy blackest night of fear,
That radiant one from heaven drew near.

The Prioress their betrothal heard,
The offer, and responsive word ;
And, calm—as was that evening hour—
Came to them from the leafy bower:
" May angels have ye in their keeping,
Save ye from sickness sad, and weeping,
And all the ills that to me clung,
For I was widow'd very young.
But Margaret, come with me away,
Lovers, at sunset, love delay ;
This night I in the castle stay,
At morn return to Lymbroke dale."
" Thither," she answer'd, " I retire,
To add my singing to the choir
Of the kind sisters of the vale."

And here I might my story close
While these two go to seek repose,

And linger there, the lovers glad ;
But in yon tower a captive sad
Is musing o'er his woes :
To his hard fate I now attend,
Before my varied song I end.
Llewellyn, by his captor brought
The eve before, to Dinan's fort,
Had heard that morn in warder's room,
By the stern Prince, pronounced his doom.
A heavy ransom he must pay,
Or pine in prison life away ;
So he was cast, his arms unbound,
Into a dungeon underground,
The lowest floor within the keep ;
Gaoler alone could hear him weep ;
So massive were the walls of stone,
No one without could hear him groan.

He there a whole day mourn'd his lot,
And time's divisions nigh forgot,
For he saw only rays of light
At intervals shed on his night
When the gruff warder rais'd a plank,
And through the opening cast his meal,
Letting a gleam of daylight steal
Down to his dungeon, dark and dank.
To the unheeding walls he mourn'd :
"Here many have to dust return'd,
It may be mine their fate to share,
Worn out by famine and despair."

He laid him down on the damp stone,
His comrades crawling things alone,—
The cold and loathsome newt and frog,—
And with his glance search'd the dark fog.
"Would I could hear but one low sigh,
To hint some human captive nigh,
For though I could not see his face
'Twould be a comfort in this place.
Without companion I must die,
Or madden, and in frenzy rave,
Fretting in this dim dismal cave.
The sun may set or have arisen,
The lark may sing, the owlet cry,
The azure fields may smile on high,
Or clouds scud through the gloomy sky,—
'Tis all the same in this dark prison."

Wearied by thought at length he slept,
But wakened, for a light foot stepp'd
Upon the floor above his head;—
Listen! it was a quiet tread,
And rustling of a woman's dress
Sweeping the floor her footsteps press;
A gentle hand then lifts the lid,
Which daylight from the dungeon hid,
And now shoot down some slanting beams
From taper, that above him gleams;
And now is heard a soft sweet voice,
"If thou wilt with some danger cope,
To leave thy cell rests in thy choice;

Look up ! and seize this hempen rope,
It to this floor is firmly fixed,
And lift thyself to where I stand."
With hope and fear and wonder mixed
He heard the kind command,
Express'd in such a gentle tone,
And seeming not to him unknown.

The taper small did ill afford
Light to disclose the dangling cord;
Five times he search'd with effort vain
The strong and helpful rope to gain,
At length he grasp'd it, and from gloom
Rais'd himself up to vaulted room.
And O what vision met his eyes !
As one who enters Paradise
After a death of suffering sad,
Looks on some dear one, and is glad,
So he beheld the features sweet
Of Margaret, waiting him to greet.
Such an angelic shape awoke
St. Peter, and his fetters broke,
And set him from his prison free.
" Breathe not a word, but follow me,"
She whisper'd; "my hand holds the key
Of every iron lock that bars
Thy vision from the moon and stars."
She put her finger to her lips,
" Hush ! answer not, pursue my steps."

N

He follow'd her small twinkling lamp
Along a narrow passage damp,
Until they reach'd the oaken door,
Studded with nail and iron clamp;
A warder at the sill did snore,
And flagon in his grasp retain'd,
Whence he the potent mead had drain'd,
Drinking the health of youthful bride
He little dream'd stood at his side!
She softly turn'd the key in lock,
And, stepping o'er the living block,
Llewellyn, glad in heart, discern'd
The moon's calm, soft, and silvery ray,
Which dazzled, as the light of day,
Him, from dark cell return'd.

They came into the castle-yard,
Where slumber'd many of the guard,
Some on their faces, some supine,
Drunk with strong ale, or mead, or wine;
For they had revell'd at the feast
In honour of the marriage day,
And though the rite was stay'd, ne'er ceas'd
To drink the hours away.
Fearing to rouse them from their sleep,
Llewellyn and his guide did creep
Across the plot of greensward, spread
With flowers, shaken from the dancer's head.
The hounds within their kennels stay'd,

For well they knew the gentle maid ;
Or came, and round her fawn'd and play'd.

Amid such signs of feast and sport
She went and ope'd the sally-port,
And they descended rock-hewn stair
Into the tilt-yard's moonlit space ;
Then turning full on him her face,
She spake with solemn air :
"While night and slumber aid escape,
Flee, and thy journey homeward shape."
It seem'd as if he heard her not,
Or hearing, stood rooted to the spot.
Charm'd by her tone, while he did linger,
His glance fell on her slender finger,
And round it, no gold ring was set ;
"So thou hast not thy lover wed,
Who thee to Dinan's altar led !"
With accent of surprise he said.
"Our union wondrous hindrance met ;
We found we were too near allied,—
I could not be my brother's bride."
"Oh ! then once more thy hand is free."
He from his bosom drew a bud,
"Thou gav'st me this in Whitcliffe wood,
My tears its leaves have oft bedew'd ;
It tells my constant love to thee ;
My heart has been, and will be true.
The foe my sire at Evesham slew,
Now I am lord of Bradwen hall,

And moor, and fields, round Idris' height;
Thou shalt be mistress of them all
If thou wilt share my flight."

"I must return the same response
To thy appeal I utter'd once;
My heart is to Another given—
Henceforth I am the bride of Heaven."
"Oh! wilt thou take a novice' hood
While May is warm within thy blood?
The world doth need such souls of light
To make its sorry scene more bright."
"My vow can never be recall'd;
Thy love for me hath been forestall'd
By One who loved me ere my birth;
I seek a home, but not of earth."
The strong youth trembled, as the weak,
And anguish'd looks his grief bespeak.

She with determined effort crush'd
The pity stirring in her heart,
The passion that her features flush'd:
"Oh! choose," she said, "the better part,
And if thou wilt wed none beside
Me, whom thou long hast wooed for bride,
Then let me be once more thy guide,—
Go, in some holy house abide;
Many such homes, with beauteous fanes,
Our lovely border-land contains:
Due prayer the monks of Wigmore make,

Beside their calm and silvery lake ;
In the gold valley Abbey Dore
Sends up her sweet hymns evermore,
And by the Honddu's rapid flood
Llanthony trains her brotherhood ;
And Tintern lifts her arches high
Upon the bank of winding Wye ;—
But if thou choosest not to roam
So far from thy dear mountain home,
Let hymns be sung and prayers be said
In holy Cymmer's hazel shade.
Yes, in some cloister calm and still,
Learn to subdue to God thy will ;
And, when our hearts have ceased to beat,
And we have reach'd the bright world yonder,
And at our far-off sorrows wonder,
We there in love may meet."

A strange unearthly beauty crept
O'er her pale face, her passions slept,
But tears of sympathy she wept ;
And, as for ever she withdrew,
Put forth her hand to bid Adieu,—
" Farewell, and think of me no more,
For soon I pass the convent-door."
With fervent touch her hand he grasp'd ;
Only a moment was it clasp'd,
When she drew back her palm, and sped
Where the fort-walls a shadow spread,
And scaled the steps cut in the rock,

And he beheld her snowy smock
Vanishing through the postern gate,
And felt how bitter was his fate.
A plaintive look he upward cast:
"Oh! yonder chaste moon is surpass'd,
And I have lost a star to-night
Than all yon stars more pure, more bright."

A cloud swam o'er the moon's calm face,
And caused a darkness for a space;
A restless owlet gave a scream,
And glided by on pinion white;
The otter splash'd in Onny stream,
The bat renew'd her circling flight.
Then on Llewellyn fell a fear;
The guard may waken, and anon
Discover that their captive's gone.
Oh! life to youth is dear:
He fled as if by foe pursued,
Dash'd through the Teme, into the wood;
Slunk, like a wolf, up Downton dell,
And when the dawn did shades dispel
Drank deep at Brampton's fairy well;
But ne'er his panic-terror lost
Till he the dyke of Offa cross'd.

He journey'd over Werry fell;
At Carreg's village Cross
Had to an anxious crowd to tell
Of Cambria's cruel loss.

Caersus's ruined Roman walls
Were reach'd when evening twilight falls;
One ope'd his door, and led him in,
Where he might rest his weary feet,
And set before him mead, and meat,
And tale of Evesham's woe did bin.
The daughters of the house then play'd
Their harps, and welcome music made;
And kindly show'd the way-worn guest
A fern-strewn pallet for his rest.
And there the youth in love so cross'd
Thought of the treasure he had lost.

At morn he started for the west,
And on his left saw mountain breeze
Stirring of heather, purple seas,
Below Plinlimmon's crest.
In fair Machynlleth's stony street,
A harp beside his knee,
A bard sate on a granite seat
In robe of minstrelsy;
Dilated eye and bristling hair
The terror of his soul declare.
Women and men around him throng,
The sacred Awen sign they know,—
See how his aged features glow!
They listen for his song.
He dash'd his hand among the strings,
And wondrous music forth he brings,
And this prophetic lay he sings.

"THE BARD'S SONG.

" How my spirit sank, afraid !
When our spearmen march'd to aid
Haughty Montfort, making boast
He would vanquish Edward's host.

"Ah ! the cowards basely fled,
But the blood of some was shed ;
Better had they all been slain,
Than their rocky mountains gain.

"Blood bedew'd the monks' abode,
Red the silvery Avon flow'd ;
But the wrath of Edward woke,
And a dreadful word he spoke—

" 'Some escape my anger now,
But they soon shall feel my blow ;
In their land I will require,
For this insult, vengeance dire.'

" Ah ! he comes, our homes to burn,
Woe to them who now return ;
Oh ! the ills that shall be borne
From the hour they rous'd his scorn.

"Now I see his onset fierce,
How the shafts our hauberks pierce ;

Now to my affrighted ear
Come the cries of grief and fear.

" Blood is in our Llyns and streams,
O'er our flesh the eagle screams.
Such a havoc Edward makes !
Such a horrid vengeance takes !"

"Oh ! his cruel sword is sharp—
Slays the minstrel by his harp ;
May I rest within the tomb
Ere shall come that day of gloom."

Thus by a sacred madness moved,
Over the cords his fingers roved—
The bard sang his ecstatic lay.
More sad, Llewellyn went his way.
One lent at Dovey's stream a boat
Of woven ozier, bound with hide,
That light as autumn's leaf did float,
And bore him o'er the tide.
He travell'd down that river's dale,
And pass'd into Dysynni's vale,
Where the wild birds of ocean flock
At eve, to Craig-y-Deryn's rock,
Then scaled Trawsfynydd's heathery hill.
Oh ! what a joy his soul did thrill,
When, from its top, he sent his glance
Over the Mawddach's broad expanse,
And mark'd Caer Idris' mountain rise,

With triple summit, to the skies.
Within Llys Bradwen's hall, alone,
He play'd his harp, but vain the tone
A consolation to impart.
Fair scenes of nature touched his heart :
He heard the sounds of Arthog's flood,
Foaming and thundering through the wood ;
But vain were all to heal his smart.
Away from Margaret's loveliness,
His life became a weariness.
He sought the pleasure of the chase,
And oft his horn would echoes wake
By lone Gregennan's wind-swept lake ;
But naught her image could efface.
It haunted him on mountain rude,
Whereon the Meini Hirion stood ;
And ever with the hunter stray'd ;
When clambering Llyn Gader's rocks,
Where scarce can climb wild goat or fox ;
Ascending Mynidd Moel high,
Round which the jagged lightnings fly ;
In knee-deep fern of Aran glen,
In the pursuit of wolf or deer,
He thought upon her words again,—
Her gentle voice rung in his ear :
" Go ; in a cloister calm and still
Learn to subdue to God thy will,
And when our hearts have ceas'd to beat,
And we have reach'd the bright world yonder,
And at our far-off sorrows wonder,

We there in love may meet."
Oh ! could he thus become more lowly,
Worthy to meet that maiden holy
Upon the far-off sunny shore,
Where sin can touch the soul no more.
That goal gleam'd alway in his sight,
Allured his mind, by day and night ;
Enthusiasm rais'd the veil,
And show'd, beyond this world of care,
Her face, by vigils now made pale,
Transform'd to be more fair ;
But soon as Awen harps did ring
And bard the savage hymn did sing
For warfare with the English king,
He bravely joined the native ranks,
And conquer'd on dark Conway's banks,—
In many a dreadful battle strove ;
But when the lance of Gwynedd broke,
And Snowdon pass'd 'neath Edward's yoke,
He yielded to his ancient love
For her, whose image ever pass'd
Before his mind ; and went at last,
When twenty summers with their glow
Had melted twenty winters' snow,
And crown'd Caer Idris with a wreath
Of golden gorse, and purple heath,
Into the Abbey of Cwm Hir,—
(Since it to Lymbroke's house was near,)—
Assumed the grey Cistercian dress,
And spent a life of holy fear

In wild Mellenyth's calm recess;
Making his better self more strong,
While rocks resounded his sweet song.

For Margaret still wore serge and hood
In Lymbroke's tranquil valley deep,
And daily broke its drowsy sleep
With hymns to Him Who hung on Rood;
And Isabel—who once had thought,
When Walter sailed to Syrian realm,
To cut her raven-tresses short,
And set on them a helm,
And follow him across the brine
To battle-fields in Palestine—
With her companion dear prevail'd
To let her share her toil divine,
Nor with her lover sail'd.

But he came back with flower-wreath'd sword,
And laurel garland on his crest,
To reap for valour rich reward,
And make that true one blest.
He brought for her a bough of palm
That waved in Jordan's valley warm;
And for his sister, rose, from stem
That grew near well of Bethlehem;
Reminding of the love and truth
Of the young gentle-hearted Ruth.
This happen'd when on double wing
Of day and night ten years did bring

To Whitcliffe wood, again, the spring.
Blithely St. Lawrence' bells did ring,
The little fortress-chapel round
Again with garlands gay was crown'd,
Woven by hand of Margaret,
Who left her cell that morning-tide,
And came, and fragrant chaplet set
Upon the forehead of the bride.

Sweet were the joys of Isabel;
More sweet for her who chose to dwell
In Lymbroke vale, in peaceful cell.
Day after day their church-bell rang,
And sweeten'd all the vale serene;
And holy hymns the sisters sang,
Telling of joys beyond this scene.
At last they sang, when pass'd the soul
Of her who held o'er them control;
And Margaret, made Prioress,
Ruled o'er the house with zeal no less
Than she whose soul from earth had gone,
And crown of heavenly honour won.
Sweet thoughts of that dear mother, dead,
Came to her, on her pallet-bed,
And seem'd as if they counsel gave
From happy worlds beyond the grave;
So comforted, she lov'd to go
And pray beside the couch of woe.

But years of youth and womanhood

Go swiftly by in doing good.
When Margaret's locks had turn'd to grey,
As she sate in her cell one day,
And saw a summer-sunset's sheen
Gilding the orchard-foliage green,
It seem'd a voice said, " Come away ; "
The tone was more than earthly sweet.
She knew that in Cwm Hir's retreat
Llewellyn's warfare was complete ;
That he who long the cloister trod
Had found the perfect peace of God,—
That he, who tried God's ways to trace,
Had gone to see Him face to face.

She long'd to cast her burden down,
And go up also to her crown ;
And, at the welcome call, fell sick.
Her pain increas'd, her pulse beat quick,
And hot with fever grew her head ;
Angels, she thought, stood round her bed ;
She seem'd to hear, by Seraph's tongue,
A Gloria in Excelsis sung ;
And when the bell for vespers rung,—
At hour which she had lov'd so well,—
Her soul ascended from her cell,
And knit an endless bond of love
With him she met in realms above.

Some said they saw a golden light
Float down from heaven's pure azure height,

And on the convent roof alight,
And then float up to heaven again,
Accompanied by a wondrous strain
Of harmony, so sweet to hear,
It always linger'd on the ear ;
And that the lady's soul was there
Borne by an angel through the air.
The nuns the virgin body laid
Beside her mother, in a tomb,
There, oft, they silent stood, and pray'd,
There left their wreaths of bloom.

Ye who have listen'd to the song
I shaped the Radnor hills among,
Go, when the rays of sunset fall
Upon that convent's crumbling wall,
And think of all the holy throng
Who brought their woes and passions there,
And soothed them by the might of prayer,
Forgetting injury and wrong.
But chiefly muse by that green mound,
Where buried lies the mortal dust
Of her on whom strange fate was thrust,
But who, the more, in God did trust,
And here a true peace found.

CHISWICK PRESS :—C. WHITTINGHAM AND CO., TOOKS COURT,
CHANCERY LANE.